NO PROMISES

MARIE HARPER WRIGHT

Jack,
Forever and always...no matter what.

CHAPTER 1

The further away from London Jodie Cook got, the better she felt. It was like a dark cloud lifting from her shoulders. She was driving with the music blaring, singing her heart out. Spring was in the air and it was one of the first days where there wasn't a need for a coat. The warm sunshine and the fresh air cleared the London smog and filled her lungs with hope.

A call came through her car speaker system. It was Kelsie, her best friend since childhood.

"Hi Kels, are you already there?" Jodie asked. There had been a bit of traffic on the way down to meet Kelsie and she was still about thirty minutes away from the village of Winton Green.

"Well…no, not exactly. I can't actually make it today."

And just like that, Jodie's mood plummeted. "What do you mean?" Her eyebrows knitted together. She had been so excited about exploring with her friend today. They didn't get to spend as much time together as they used to, now that Kelsie had children. Jodie had called her at the beginning of the week—heart racing and chewing on her thumbnail—to explain everything. And Kelsie had cancelled her weekend plans to support Jodie.

"Maisie has just thrown up everywhere. I'm so sorry. I can't leave her when she's ill."

Jodie felt her throat burn and tears try to surface but she pushed them back down. It wasn't Kelsie's fault, she would be there if she could. "I completely understand. Is she okay?"

"I'm really gutted. I have put her in my bed to rest, and she's snuggling and watching tv, bless her. I was so looking forward to today."

Jodie's heart seared at the thought of Maisie in pain. She was a sweet little girl who somehow always managed to persuade Jodie to let her do her make-up. There had been many occasions where Jodie left Kelsie's house looking like a clown.

Now there was shouting in the background.

"That's her. I have to go. I'm sorry, Jodie. Let me know how you get on." And with that, Kelsie was gone.

Jodie sighed. She didn't want to do this alone. Pressing the phone button on her steering wheel, she called the only other person she could rely on.

The robotic voice spoke to her. "Please say a command."

"Call Mum," she shouted. It was always a bit temperamental and she had to shout at it to get it to work.

"Calling Mum on mobile." Sharp dialling tones erupted from the speakers.

"Hello, sweetie," her mum Sandra replied.

"You won't believe what's happened."

"Oh dear, what? Aren't you meant to be village shopping today? I thought it would be a good day." Sandra's concern was evident in her tone.

"Yes, but Maisie has just been sick and Kelsie can't leave her." Tears threatened to spill over, but Jodie blinked them away, chiding herself for being overdramatic.

"Bless her heart. Is she okay? Does that mean you've decided to postpone?"

"No, I'm about thirty minutes out from Winton Green and I have that viewing booked. I can't afford to miss it. Mum, can you come with me?" she begged, white knuckles gripping the steering wheel. This was the biggest decision she had ever made in her life and she just wanted someone there with her.

"Oh Jodie, I would love to but I'm out with your dad. I wouldn't make it in time."

Jodie didn't speak, knowing her voice would crack if she did, but her mum sensed her panic.

"Sweetheart, it will all be okay, you can still go. Don't let this be a wasted journey. Life is too short."

"I didn't want to do this on my own," Jodie mumbled. Having Kelsie alongside her to be her sounding board would have just made her decision that much easier, or at least she'd hoped it would.

"I know, sweetie. Kelsie would be with you if she could, but it can't be helped. You have two choices, don't you?" Sandra prompted.

"No," she sulked, just wanting to wallow in self-pity.

"Jodie…"

She didn't need to see her mum to know her eyebrows would be raised, her foot tapping away impatiently. It was as if Jodie were a teenager again. Like the time that she and Kelsie each pretended they were having a sleepover at the other's house, when in reality they went to a party and slept in a tent in someone's back garden. Jodie still didn't know how her mum had found out, but the memory of the look on her face when she strode through the front door the next morning still made her blood run cold.

"Yes, Mother. I can go anyway or return home." Looked like her wallowing would have to wait. She was acting like a teenager and she knew it. She shook herself and pulled her shoulders back.

"And what are you going to choose to do?" Sandra prompted again.

"I'm going to go anyway. I'm too close to turn around." She held onto that sliver of hope that clung to her heart. This was her chance. This was her opportunity. To finally hand back the life that had been handed to her, the life she had never really wanted. To finally be brave. If she couldn't do this on her own, how did she expect to move here and set up a business on her own?

"Good girl."

Jodie could hear the smile in Sandra's voice. At that exact moment, she knew her mum was proud of her. That tiny sliver of hope grew to a shard.

"Park up and have a drink at the pub, have a little look around and go from there," Sandra said. "You never know, maybe this is your destiny. Positive thoughts have positive outcomes. You are strong and brave, believe it."

Her words of wisdom hung in the air. She was right. Jodie could do this.

She took a deep breath, the threat of earlier tears forgotten and determination replacing her panic. "Love you Mum." Crisis averted.

"Remember Jodie, feel the fear. Then do it anyway."

Tony Wade shoved his shoes on, exasperated. He was hopping from one foot to the other making a fool out of himself. Luckily only Max, his faithful spaniel, was there to see him. The one lazy morning he had at home and it was ruined. Yet again he was needed at the local pub. *His pub.*

He grabbed the plastic bag at the front door and let Max

out in front of him. Blowing out a frustrated breath, he commanded his shoulders to drop an inch or two as he counted to ten. He shouldn't be annoyed. This was what happened in pubs. Especially when you hired kids straight out of college or sixth form.

The village of Winton Green had been his home for five years now. He had worked hard here, every minute of every day, never giving up on realising his dream. He was the landlord of The Dog. It was the quintessential country pub, the heart of the community, serving real ales, good food and a friendly atmosphere. Its white brick walls, aging beams and creaky floorboards had been here for hundreds of years.

Tony had finally accomplished his goal of owning his own pub five years ago. Five years of hard work, sleepless nights and hair pulling. Now, as he inspected the planters at the front of the pub filled with English lavender and soon-to-be-blooming tulips, he knew the hard work would never stop.

A nagging feeling rumbled deep within his stomach, something he hadn't felt for a long time. He needed something more. Sighing, he looked up at his livelihood, muscles tense and aching.

That nagging, grumbling pain wouldn't go away until he did something. Something new and exciting. Something he hadn't done before. He'd had that same incessant, niggling feeling in the pit of his stomach seven years ago. That was when his dream of owning a pub had really started. He'd had that same nagging feeling at university and had decided to swap his degree to business management. And then again when he knew it was time to get a dog.

Every time, it brought him somewhere new—a new project to concentrate on, a new task to fulfil. Until finally he had moved to Winton Green. Welcomed in by a community he didn't know, he'd created the beauty that stood before him. Maybe it was time to convert the top rooms of the pub into a B&B, like he had initially thought about.

A shrill ringing interrupted the peaceful green. He looked at the caller ID on his phone and sighed heavily. His mum. He still hadn't returned her call from the last time she rang. She would have to wait…again.

"Max," he called out. "Come on, boy."

The chocolate-brown spaniel came straight to him, loyal and loving as ever. He'd got Max four years ago, as a puppy. Even though he was always surrounded by people in the pub, a loneliness had crept up on him—one that he couldn't shake.

When he first met puppy Max, he'd had those big loving eyes, and unlike his brothers and sisters who were jumping up for attention, Max sat staring at him, his tail wagging, his soppy eyes boring into Tony's own. They had gone into a separate room to see if they were a match and Tony had fallen in love. Max snuggled up close to him enjoying the love and affection. When Tony got up off the floor to speak to the breeder, Max followed him and sat next to his feet, staring up in adoration. They'd been together ever since.

Max had been sniffing the bushes and plants as if also inspecting them. Who was he kidding? Knowing Max, he had probably buried a bone in one, the little rascal. His nose was muddy from his inspection. Tony wiped it off, smiling down at the little bump he'd had on his nose since he was a pup. Then they headed inside, Tony carrying the plastic bag and Max wagging his tail happily.

"John, think fast," he shouted and threw the bag to the barman, his best friend. Max nudged Tony with his wet nose, as if reading his mind and reminding him. Okay, Max was his best friend and John a close second.

John was growing his beard out and was just getting past the itchy, patchy stage and was looking more presentable now. Tony teased him about it every day, but he had to admit, the dark covering suited him. John was opening the bag he'd caught.

"Don't say I never get you anything," Tony called back to him as he walked to the open brick fireplace.

"Nice one, Tony!" John beamed, genuinely happy with his gift of three new stripy tea towels. John without a tea towel slung over his shoulder or in his hand was a rare sight. Looking like a kid who'd got an early Christmas present, he chucked a new towel over his shoulder and deposited the others underneath the bar for safekeeping.

Tony lit the fire sitting in pride of place in the pub. It was the thing he'd fallen most in love with about the place when he was buying it. And now he loved being the one to organise the logs and kindling and get the fire roaring. When it was lit, the crackling fire made The Dog feel cosy—a home from home.

Having John on board had been a life-saver. Not only was he an excellent bar manager, but in turn he had become Tony's closest friend. With John around, Tony didn't need to spend as much time at the pub as he had done when he first bought it. He didn't really have anything else to occupy his time, so if he wasn't working the bar, he was usually mingling with the patrons—both new and regular—ensuring his hard work didn't slip through his fingers and fail like a lot of pubs did these days.

Unfortunately, John couldn't sort out the staffing problem. That was Tony's domain. "Where's Micha?" he asked John as he watched the fire take hold before him, spreading to the logs, already warming his skin.

"In the kitchen, I think," John replied, wiping down the bar once more, rolled-up sleeves showing his tattooed arms.

Tony got up from the floor and went to find Micha. That nagging feeling returned. What on earth did it want him to do?

"Micha?" he called into the industrial kitchen. Max knew he wasn't allowed in, so he settled himself at the door, waiting for his owner to return. Stainless steel worktops and appliances sparkled. It was quiet now, but the chefs would soon arrive to prepare for the lunchtime rush and the place would be a cacophony of chopping, sautéing and shouting.

"Alright, Tony," she called back, her Afro blowout bouncing as she turned. Micha was his second in command for the restaurant and ran a tight ship to ensure customers came from miles around to dine at The Dog. "What do you want me to do with Chloe's resignation?"

Their latest recruit had just been offered her dream job at the local estate agents and was starting straight away. So now they were short-staffed...again. All the staff at The Dog were like a family, and they would all be happy for Chloe. But her leaving meant closing ranks again and everyone going above and beyond to cover the gaping hole in shifts.

"Are we able to cover her hours in the short term at least?" Tony asked, rubbing the stubble on his chin.

"Should be able to. But the guys will quickly get burnt out again. It hasn't been that long since the last girl left and they had to cover that hole too." She raised her perfectly pencilled eyebrows.

"I know." He ran his hands through his hair. "I'll cover anything that needs to be covered, don't worry."

"I know you will. God forbid you have a night off and sit with your feet up!" Micha replied sarcastically before walking out into the dining area. He followed, nabbing a bit of cheese on the way out for Max to have as a treat.

"How busy are we?" he asked as Max gently took the cheese.

"Very. We need a long-term solution, Tony."

"I know. I'm trying." He sighed.

"I know." She patted him on the back as she left.

CHAPTER 2

The Satnav had successfully guided Jodie to Winton Green, a quaint little village all centred around a triangular green. Bright yellow and white daffodils bordered the green and there were matching cottages surrounding all three sides, with cricket stumps still in the middle, just waiting for the next match to be played.

According to her research, the local pub, The Dog, was well known around the area and had become a go-to place to eat and drink in recent years. An old-fashioned corner shop sat at the other end of the green—the type that probably still had a little bell above the door that chimed whenever anyone entered.

She parked her car and stretched her legs, clad in her funky, black, wetlook leggings. Her white blouse rose up as she stretched her arms above her head. The healing sunshine warmed her skin as she breathed in the fresh air, absorbing all its strength.

Following her mother's advice, she strode to the pub, her high-heeled boots tapping and echoing off the cottages. She would have a drink first, gather her thoughts and make a little action plan of her own. Then get her butt in gear.

Pulling her shoulders back and plastering a confident smile on her face, she pushed open the heavy door and was greeted with the usual chatter of a pub. Instead of the stuffy, old-fashioned pub she had been expecting, this was bright and friendly with country industrial vibes. The ceilings still held their original beams and dark wooden cladding surrounded the bottom two thirds of the walls, painted in a dark grey. A large, open, brick fireplace stood in the middle, separating the space into two drinking areas. There was an eclectic mix of wooden tables and chairs, and large, comfy leather armchairs next to the roaring fire.

She snapped herself out of gawking at the interior design and walked to the bar. A friendly barman walked over to serve her, with dark hair and swirling tribal tattoos that spread across his forearms. "Welcome to The Dog. What can I get for you?"

She rustled around in her bag for her purse. "A Coke would be great, please."

He went about pouring her drink as she observed the locals. There was a mixture of people—family groups, walkers, older couples and a group of tall, gorgeous men standing around the large brick fireplace. The clattering of cutlery echoed from the diners at the back of the pub.

Twisting through the crowds with her drink in hand, she found a wooden table off to one side with a mismatched armchair. Perfect. She settled herself down, checking the time on her phone. She wouldn't have long here, but enough to get a feel for the place.

Excitement started bubbling in her tummy, so much so that she could have let out a little shriek. But sitting alone in a pub, where she was surrounded by strangers, it was probably best to keep that shriek in. She couldn't put her finger on it, but something about this place seemed right, made her excited for her future. And to think she'd almost turned around because Kelsie wasn't able to come with her.

She took a sip of her cold Coke, the ice clinking in the glass from her shaking hand. She had to stay calm, keep a level head. She had hardly seen any of what Winton Green had to offer, but already this was the nicest village she had visited. Maybe it had something to do with the spring sunshine, or the friendly locals. But she just felt a vibe that this was the place she was meant to be. Thank God she had listened to her mum. Could this just be the place?

She pulled up the pictures on her phone of the house again. It was by far her favourite that she'd seen online. A quaint little cottage right on the green. It was a bit outdated, definitely in need of sprucing up. But hey, that was her speciality, right?

Deep, hearty laughs erupted from the group of men by the fireplace, drawing her attention away from her phone. Although all the men were handsome, she was drawn to one man who had his back to her. He was wonderfully tall and toned, and had chocolate-brown hair styled short on the sides, the top longer and swept back. His back was strong and muscular, and his biceps tugged at his polo shirt. If only he would just turn around and she could see what he really looked like.

She pictured him as the most attractive man she'd ever seen. But surely men *that* good-looking didn't exist. There had to be something wrong with him. He probably had dodgy teeth, or a squeaky voice.

He laughed again, the sound landing right between her thighs and making her all mushy inside. Nope, definitely not a squeaky voice.

A beautiful brown cocker spaniel sat obediently next to him. The dog had a little bump on his otherwise straight nose and his fur matched the colour of the man's hair perfectly.

As soon as Jodie made eye contact with the handsome young dog, he wagged his tail and sauntered over to where she sat. His owner immediately noticed his movement and stared after him. And Jodie couldn't stop looking at the man. Dark stubble framed his strong jaw and his piercing brown eyes were the same colour as his hair. His eyes didn't leave the dog.

∼

"Max." Tony's voice was almost thunderous. The pub was dog friendly, but that didn't mean everyone wanted a dog rushing over to them. Normally he stayed by Tony's side no matter what.

Max stopped in his tracks, just a short distance from his intended target. "He's alright," the stranger spoke out on Max's behalf. As if understanding, the dog practically jiggled across the small distance so he could get a stroke. Only at that point did Tony look up and see the beauty Max was so drawn to. Tony was lost in her eyes, which were the colour of the village green outside. Chestnut-brown curls fell just past her full breasts and she wore a shy smile on her luscious Cupid's bow lips, which were a perfect shade of rose pink.

A fire smouldered within him, fiercer than the fire he had lit that morning in the grate behind him. Breaking his stare, he called over to her, willing his voice not to crack. "He's a gentle lad, but just shout if you want him gone." Before she could reply, he turned back round to continue drinking with his buddy James and some other regulars, the exposed skin on his neck burning up at the thought she might just be staring at him at that very moment.

Trying to compose himself, he took a large gulp of his beer. He would not allow himself to look back at her.

Categorically. Under no circumstances was he going to give in. He didn't date women. They were too complicated, too demanding. There was no time in his life for one. And he sure as hell wouldn't get involved with a random woman who had just waltzed into *his* pub and *his* life unannounced.

He took another gulp of the deep copper liquid.

Who was he kidding? It was his responsibility to make sure Max behaved himself. He turned his head slightly, desperately hoping she wouldn't catch him gawping at her.

"Hello, Max," Jodie whispered down to the dog who had his head resting on her lap. Every stroke of his soft fur calmed her nerves. She sat drinking with Max sitting diligently next to her, as if keeping an eye on her. The handsome man, with his dark smouldering eyes, regularly looked round to check up on the dog. And maybe, just maybe, to stare at her too. Every time he looked, little butterflies erupted in her tummy. But he didn't make any more eye contact with her and when he turned round again the butterflies quickly flew away.

She could have sat there for hours on end, but she was procrastinating. She had come here with a purpose. A woman on a mission. Last week her employer had put everyone on notice for redundancies. They were merging with another building company and needed to reduce the number of staff. Everyone around her had been devastated at the news, worried for their jobs and livelihood. Jodie hadn't. She couldn't help but wonder, *what if*.

She'd called her mum straight away. "It sounds like an amazing opportunity, Jodie," Sandra had said after hearing her daughter out. "You sound quite excited, yet a bit hesitant?"

"I'm just waiting for someone to tell me not to," Jodie replied, biting her nails. She'd been expecting to be told how stupid she was for even contemplating taking the redundancy to set up on her own.

"Why would anyone do that?" Sandra asked her, allowing Jodie time to express herself and work through her emotions.

"Because I'd be throwing away security from a job for no security at all. What if I fail?"

"What if you succeed?" Sandra responded.

And that was what had done it. That was what had made her mind up. That was what led her here.

"Right, Max," she directed at her drinking partner. "I have stuff to do. Thank you for keeping me company." His soppy eyes stared into hers, his head tilting from one side to the other at her words as he tried to comprehend their meaning. She gave his head one last scratch and stood up.

Tony had failed miserably at not staring at the gorgeous woman behind him. Even though he kept telling himself he wasn't interested in a relationship, the woman behind him had him in a tangle like he'd never experienced before. How could he be so drawn to someone he had barely spoken to? He'd completely lost all track of the conversation happening around him, but thankfully a few laughs and nods in the right places meant the other men around him hadn't noticed.

A chair scraped behind him and the smell of spring flowers floated past as the temptress walked back to the bar. Max appeared by his side, his nose wet on Tony's hand.

"Excuse me," he said to his companions. He couldn't help himself—it was now or never and he wasn't prepared to settle for the latter. What was it about her that was so different?

Following her up to the bar, he resisted looking at her pert backside in those leather-like trousers. He hated himself for following her. His mind kept telling him this was ridiculous, to back off and leave the woman alone. But another part of him just couldn't leave her be.

As he appeared next to her, her breath hitched. A small smile tugged at his lips, the most genuine he had smiled all day. "Did he behave?" he enquired, his voice shattering the silence between them.

She looked up at him through her long eyelashes, the same pink hue of her lips spreading across her cheeks. "Of course, he's a very well-behaved dog," she responded, biting her lower lip. Great, now he wanted to do the same.

Instead, he gave Max a little 'well done' stroke. Tony was playing a dangerous game. He wanted to kiss her, bite her lip like she had, right there and then, without even knowing her name. "Good." He nodded, at a loss for words. "We'll see you around?"

"Yeah, maybe." She hesitated, as if wanting to say more. Seeming to think better of it, she turned to thank John, who was smirking at Tony like an idiot, and left. The scent of soft flowers lingered in the air.

John's eyes burned into him, that silly grin getting wider.

"What?" Tony shot at him.

"Nothing." John threw his tea towel over his shoulder and left to serve a customer, a knowing look on his face.

CHAPTER 3

Jodie breathed in the fresh air as she explored the village, her mind, body and soul suddenly invigorated. This was what the countryside was all about—the sound of silence, beautiful little cottages and sinfully gorgeous locals. She shook her head. No. Not sinfully gorgeous locals with a voice so deep it hit her straight in the chest. This was about her. About her future. And that future did not include a man. But God, he was something.

A group of walkers strode by her on the way to the pub and said 'hi' as they passed, jolting her out of her inappropriate daydream. Their friendly hello was a surprise to her, coming from London where strangers didn't interact with each other.

Clearing her mind of all thoughts of the mysterious man, she marvelled at every little sight—the little picket fences, the friendly villagers, the birds sitting in the trees chirping happily. This was exactly what she'd been wanting—what she'd been craving—for God knows how long. She had never wanted to live the life she lived in London. She'd never wanted to be part of the rat race. That life had been handed to her, and she had never been brave enough to hand it back.

It was her mum who had got her the job at Shelter, after she graduated from university. Just to keep her going till she found her dream job, hopefully something that would use her degree in interior design. But that had never happened. Jodie wasn't really sure why. Time had just passed her by so quickly and now here she was, a twenty-nine-year-old single woman with no career, no boyfriend and no life. Kelsie would say she was in a 'funk' and to snap out of it, take the bull by the horns and make changes. But like with everything else at the moment, she just didn't know where to begin.

She looked at the time on her phone. Bugger, she had five minutes to find the house. She quickly brought up the address details.

The cottage was easy enough to find, nestled between two others with the same honey-coloured bricks and a slate roof. It had a perfectly manicured garden in the front, a pale blue painted gate and a picturesque view of the green.

She breathed a deep, calming breath. *Feel the fear, then do it anyway.*

Knocking on the door, she waited with her heart in her mouth. This felt too important, like her whole life depended on it. Which it did. Well…her future anyway.

An older gentleman opened the door and smiled down at her, his eyes creasing. "Hello, young lady, what can I do for you?"

Jodie didn't think she'd ever get used to the friendly nature of people in the country. "Hi, I'm Jodie. I'm here to look at the house."

"Oh, Jodie." The man practically jumped, looking at the watch on his wrist. "We weren't expecting you for another hour yet."

"Oh, really? I thought our appointment was at one thirty."

She looked at the email on her phone again. Dread spread through every bone in her body as she read '2:30'. *What an idiot.* She suddenly felt very hot. "Oh, I'm so sorry. I must've read the time wrong. I do apologise. I'll come back in an hour." She turned to leave, mortified.

The door opened wider and a lady joined them, her grey hair perfectly styled in a trendy bob. "Hello," she said cheerily.

Before Jodie could apologise again and retreat any further, the gentleman spoke. "Jodie's here to see the house, she read the time wrong."

"Oh, I see."

"I'm so sorry, I don't know what happened. But I'll come back in an hour."

"Nonsense." The lady smiled at her. "No need for that. I'm Angie." She held out her hand for Jodie to shake. "And this is my husband Ben." Jodie shook Ben's hand too. "We're all ready for you anyway and it's not like we have to wait around for some stuffy estate agent either. Come on in." They ushered her into their home. "This is the living room." Angie took charge, for which Jodie was glad.

It was the perfect size for two people. The ceilings weren't too low either, unlike in some traditional houses. The decoration was quite dated—magnolia covered the walls and the blue carpet had seen a lot of wear over the years. Their furniture was an eclectic mix of items they had probably picked up at different stages of their life.

Angie said, "Even though it's on the green, the village is so quiet you don't hear any traffic or noise, do you Ben?" He shook his head.

Floral curtains hung at the window. Jodie peered out onto the front garden and the green beyond. It was lovely and sunny, just the right place to install a window seat. The focal point of the room was the brick fireplace right in the centre of the far wall.

When Jodie wandered over there, Ben said, "The fire works."

"Yes, it's lovely in the winter, cuddled around the fire with blankets," Angie added.

Jodie smiled at them. Like everything in this village so far, they made her feel at ease. "I can imagine." She looked around the room. "How long have you lived here?"

"Goodness me, a long time. Is it about thirty years now, Ben?" Angie asked her husband. He nodded in agreement.

"Really, thirty years?"

"We've loved every moment of it," Ben said, smiling at Angie from across the room, his eyes twinkling.

"Why move now then?" Jodie asked, slightly confused.

"We've had our life here, now it's time for something new," Angie said. "Our son lives further away than we would like. He wants us to move into a granny annexe so we can be close to them and the grandkids. We thought long and hard, and finally decided to do it."

"We're going to travel the country first though, while the annexe is being completed. Enjoy our last bit of freedom." Ben winked at Angie, who gave a little laugh.

"Through here is the kitchen." Angie directed her through the door in the back wall.

The kitchen had plenty of work space and they had placed a little dining table along one wall. The cabinets were a dark wood, with white countertops. A beautiful, old-fashioned farmhouse sink sat underneath the kitchen window looking out onto the back garden. With a lick of paint, new handles and a nice wooden countertop, the place would feel transformed.

"Ben does all the gardening here. He's created a lovely little space out the back." Angie opened up a stable barn door, split into two with a little curtained window in the top section.

"I love the door." Jodie practically skipped over to touch it.

"I always dreamed of having one," she said, her eyes glazing over with joy.

The back garden was just as stunning and immaculate as the front. A little patio area was surrounded with pots full of different coloured flowers. The garden was small, with a little grass area lined on two sides by colourful shrub borders.

"It's beautiful," Jodie complimented them. At the back of the garden was a low fence overlooking a little field. She instinctively walked towards it. "What a lovely view."

"Isn't it just? It makes the washing up a bit more enjoyable," Ben said.

Angie raised one questioning eyebrow. "Does it now? Then how come you never wash up?" She crossed her arms, looking at him. He had no response, and Angie laughed at him and continued, "Come on dear, let's show you upstairs. So where do you currently live, Jodie?"

"I live in a flat in London," she replied, following them up the creaky staircase.

"Do you really?" Angie said. "That's a bit different from here. Why the change of pace?"

"Well," Jodie explained, "I've always wanted to live in the countryside and be a part of a community. The London life has never really suited me, but I got complacent at my job and never made the change. Now there are redundancies at my work and I feel like this could be my chance."

"What a lovely way to make a horrible situation good," Angie replied with a beaming smile. "What will you do for work?"

"I'm going to set up my own business. I've always wanted to do interior design and I have a degree in it, so I'm finally going to use it."

"Isn't that wonderful, Ben?"

"Very courageous, Jodie," he said. "Setting up my own

business was the best thing I ever did to support my family. With hard work and dedication, anything is possible."

Upstairs, they showed her the two bedrooms and bathroom. The bathroom was very old-fashioned, with a blue bath nestled underneath the window, and there was no shower. She had expected some work, and replacing a bathroom down the line wasn't a worry to her. Kelsie's husband Mark would be able to help. With a bit of painting and tiling, a new suite and a shower, this place would be luxurious.

"Your house is lovely." Jodie looked over the green from the master bedroom. This place fit her. Not the decor and furniture, and there was work to be done to every room in the house. But it was liveable and a project she would gladly take on. This cottage had been a home to Ben and Angie—maybe it could be a home to her too. This house, this village, felt familiar to her. It felt right. It felt like home.

"How much are you hoping to get?" she asked. She was probably meant to be nonchalant about showing interest, to haggle and get a good deal. But she wasn't that way inclined, and in the short time she had spent with Ben and Angie, she felt they were owed more than that.

They looked at each other. "Two hundred and forty thousand," Angie said.

Jodie nibbled her lip. Although property prices were cheaper here than in London, it was a sought-after area, enough to mean she'd need a small mortgage. She loved this village already, she hadn't found a lot of properties online to view, and none of the ones she had seen so far had made her even a tad as excited as this one did.

"We'll go and make a hot drink and you come down when you're finished. Feel free to keep looking around." Angie gave Jodie's arm a little rub of reassurance.

"A coffee would be great, thank you."

They left and Jodie stood statue-still overlooking the green, her mind racing a hundred miles a second. This did seem like fate. But it also seemed too good to be true. But was it? Was it silly just to jump into it? She went back and forth. What if she couldn't afford to live here while building up a business? What if she failed?

Her mum's sentiment came back to her in that moment. *What if you succeed?*

Her body zinged at the realisation. This could be where her life started. This could be her home, her business and her future. Ben had called her courageous, but she hadn't ever been brave before. Maybe this was unleashing a new side to her that had been hidden in the smog of London. Feel the fear…then do it anyway.

She rushed downstairs to the kitchen, walking in on Ben and Angie who were whispering in hushed tones.

"Thank you for showing me around."

"Not at all, it's a pleasure to have you here." Angie handed her a steaming mug of coffee. They sat at the table and Jodie nursed her cup, breathing in the aroma, the awkwardness returning. *Just be brave.*

"Would you consider selling your home to me?" She could have said more, about how much she loved the property, the area, or even try to haggle on price. But she sensed a connection between her, the property, and Ben and Angie, and hoped they felt it too.

Their faces broke out into big beaming smiles. "We would love to," they both said at the same time.

The relief shot out of Jodie. "Really?" she asked, bewildered by their quick response.

"Of course." Angie took her hand and squeezed it. "I know we don't know you, but we feel like this could be your home and make you as happy as it made us."

"Here, here," Ben said, raising his cup in agreement.

Jodie smiled through the tears trickling down her cheeks. "Thank you so much."

"Just promise us one thing." Ben leant forward over the table towards her.

"What's that?" she asked.

"When you decide to move on from this place, you'll sell it to someone who will love it as much as we all have."

Jodie nodded in agreement, smiling.

"Shall we go for a celebratory drink at The Dog?" Angie suggested. "We can sit and sort everything out with Jodie."

"That would be lovely. Thank you." Jodie was astounded at the day's events. Sure, there was a long way to go, what with solicitors and getting a mortgage. And yes, it was all happening quickly.

But it just felt right.

CHAPTER 4

Tony had carried on drinking with John, James and Adam. They were all roughly the same age, and normally when they got together, they laughed and joked like schoolkids.

Tony was even close to John's sister, Sophie. And Adam's sister Belle also drank in the pub and just so happened to be Sophie's best friend. Sophie was like a sister to him, and both he and John were fiercely protective of her. Especially when it came to her good-for-nothing boyfriend.

Now James was telling them his latest conquest story. Tony had no idea how he did it, but James seemed to spend every night with a different woman. Sure, Tony had had his fair share of one-night stands, but now he wondered what it all meant. Normally he would egg James on, but now he was too distracted to listen. Too distracted by thoughts of that woman. The nagging feeling had settled itself firmly in the bottom of his stomach.

Max moved next to him, disappearing again. What had gotten into him today? Tony grew uneasy. Maybe he was poorly? This was so out of character for him.

Tony turned to find him and to his delight, Max was sitting

next to the beautiful stranger again, exactly where they had been before, as if she had never disappeared. Tony caught the grin before it escaped and settled on his lips. What had made her come back?

Max's big eyes stared up at her lovingly. Normally a look only reserved for Tony.

She was sitting next to Angie as Ben wandered over carrying drinks. Maybe she was their relative? They sure seemed friendly.

As if sensing someone was staring at her, she looked up at him, her eyes not showing the least bit of surprise to see it was him. Almost instantly, she gave a small, shy smile and lifted her hand slightly in an awkward little wave.

He couldn't help but send a small, shy smile back and nod at her. Then Angie took her attention back by asking a question. The loss of her gaze hit deep in the pit of his stomach. Turning back to James and the other men in the group, Tony listened to his tale, but all the time his mind was on the woman behind him, who had both him and Max in a muddle.

Ben and Angie left about thirty minutes later, but the unknown beauty seemed to be staying put for now. Tony made his way to the bar, hoping to catch her when she did leave.

As always, John stood watching at the bar, and he walked over to where Tony was leaning, that wicked little smirk back on his face. "Something you want to ask, Tony?" He raised his eyebrows up and down, mocking his friend.

"Nope." Tony turned his back on John and leant against the bar, not wanting to give him the satisfaction of seeing he was getting to him. It was a mistake though, as now all he wanted to do was stare at the beauty in the corner stroking his dog and working on a tablet she must have pulled from her bag.

Man, what he would do in that moment to swap places with Max. He turned back around with a sigh.

"You sure?" John asked.

"Certain," Tony replied. He could not be losing his head over some stranger.

"Suit yourself." John smiled over his shoulder, but Tony didn't need that cue to tell him she was approaching—he could already smell her perfume, hear her light footsteps getting closer, and feel the energy vibrate around him as she neared.

He took a steadying drink of his beer as she joined him at the bar, Max between them. "Thanks, John," she said, depositing glasses down on the bar top.

"My pleasure." He stood there grinning like a class clown, staring back and forth between Tony and the beauty, obviously enjoying their awkwardness.

Tony would pay for this for weeks, he knew it. "Max hasn't been any trouble, has he?" he asked her, his eyes locked on the back wall of the bar. He didn't trust himself to look at her—he knew he'd get lost in her eyes and might never find his way back.

"Not at all," she said. Unable to resist, he turned and met her gaze. His stomach bubbled with nervous excitement. What on earth was she doing to him? She stroked Max's tufty hair again and added, "He's been very good company."

"He doesn't usually leave my side. He must really like you." Tony tucked his hands into his tight jean pockets. When he stood tall, she came to about his shoulders.

She smiled down at Max, love in her eyes. "Well, I have to leave now." She stopped and nibbled on her lower lip, looking like she wanted to say something more. "I might see you around."

"Yeah, see you around," he said. Part of him wanted to act, to make a move, but the other part reminded himself that he didn't date. Long ago, he'd decided that settling down and a happily ever after wasn't for him. He'd seen what happened when you settled for life. And he'd be happier without it. No, this woman was dangerous. A distraction he couldn't afford. A distraction he didn't want.

He watched her walk toward the door. "Max, stay," he commanded.

She turned around and looked down at Max. Tony knew the look that would be on the dog's face, his big puppy dog eyes staring and begging her to stay. He wasn't entirely sure his eyes didn't say the same thing. Without looking back up at him, she turned and left.

He was sure he'd never see her again. Maybe that wasn't a bad thing.

John shuffled closer to him again.

"Don't say a word," Tony warned him, and drained his beer. He wanted nothing more than to wipe the smirk off John's face, and John knew it.

"I wasn't going to say anything." And he picked up the empty glasses and left.

CHAPTER 5

Max ran around Tony's heels, sniffing the ground, excited at all the smells around him. You'd think it was his first time visiting the stream, but it wasn't. They came here practically every other day. They were creatures of habit.

Tony sat on his usual rock, watching Max enjoy life, finding trails of God knows what. This was one of two walks that he and Max went on, and this was the spot they normally came to when Tony wanted to sit and think. The stream trickled over the pebbles and rocks, dropping off in a little waterfall a short distance away. The sounds calmed him—the birds in the trees, the wind blowing softly over the leaves, and Max sniffing the ground.

He'd been feeling uneasy for a couple of months now, since that nagging feeling started in his stomach. Ever since that day he'd thought about setting up the B&B. The same day that beautiful woman had appeared. She may have left and never returned, but she hadn't left his thoughts.

Tony shook himself. It was the B&B that was the issue, not the woman, he tried to convince himself for the hundredth time.

The thought of setting up the B&B—the planning, the finances, the decorating, the uncertainty—filled him with dread. That was why he was procrastinating so much. Normally when he had an idea, he chucked himself into the deep end and got on with it. Like when he knew his next step in life would be owning his own pub. Sure, it had taken him two years to get the money together and find the right one, but he'd started as soon as the idea popped up in his head. But this time he felt tired just thinking about it.

Max came over to him, a stick in his mouth, tail wagging proudly. He dropped it on Tony's lap for safekeeping. "Lovely stick, boy." Tony chuckled, giving his head a little stroke, and then Max left again to find new treasures. If only Tony could be as happy as he was.

Tony had always wanted more. He was always thinking about the next thing, the next step towards whatever goal he had at the time, until finally he achieved his lifelong dream— owning his very own, successful pub. He'd thought this place was his forever, that he would be content here, doing what he was doing, for the rest of his life. Just him and Max. Now his nagging stomach told him differently.

Getting up from the rock he was perched on, he knew what he had to do. He just didn't want to do it. Stretching out his back, he whistled for Max to follow.

As they neared the village, he pulled his phone from his pocket, checking he now had signal. He scrolled through the contacts until he found her name. Blowing out his breath, he waited for her to answer.

"Hello?"

"Hi Lexi, it's Tony from The Dog at Winton Green." He had met Lexi months and months ago after she introduced herself to him at the pub. She worked for a company that advertised and endorsed independent pubs, running social media campaigns and hosting award ceremonies. She had wanted them to go for an award but he'd politely declined.

"Tony, it's so nice to hear from you. How are you? How's the pub doing?"

"Yeah, all good. I was just wondering if I could pick your brain, really. About my next venture." He slowed his pace, Max sniffing the hedges around them.

"That sounds very exciting. Don't tell me you want to go for an award?"

He chuckled. "Well, not at the moment." He paused. Although it would probably help, having an award to boost some bookings for a B&B. Maybe he'd have to keep an open mind on that one. "I've just been thinking about what else I can do at the pub, and didn't know who better to get advice from."

"What a flatterer you are, Tony." She giggled like a little girl. If she'd been standing next to him, no doubt she would have playfully hit his chest. He'd got the vibe from her that she was interested in him when they first met, and he supposed his compliment could have been misconstrued as flirting.

"I'm actually going to be away on holiday, so can we arrange something for when I'm back?"

"Of course." He scrubbed at the dirt on the ground with his boot.

"Great. I'll send you over some dates I'm available to come down. Maybe we can have dinner?"

"Yep, sounds great."

"Perfect. That's a date then. I'll speak to you soon." And she hung up before he could tell her it was just business, pure and simple. Definitely not a date. But she didn't see it that way.

He cursed under his breath, ruffling his hair in frustration. Women. This was why he was forever a bachelor. Women were trouble. He whistled for Max, ready to get home and eat, his belly growling.

Shoving the phone back in his pocket, he looked around. "Max?" There was no rustling in the bushes. He whistled again, louder this time. He must have caught wind of a rabbit. "Here, boy." Panic washed over him, the blood draining from him.

A louder whistle. Still Max did not appear. Tony's heart sank. Where had he gone? Tony hadn't been paying attention when he was on the phone. Instead he'd been too busy worrying about Lexi believing he'd asked her on a date. Cursing, he searched through some of the bushes.

Nothing. Maybe Max had wandered off home. He knew the way. Maybe he hadn't realised Tony had stopped walking, and was waiting on their doorstep. Fear pushed Tony's legs to run as he carried on whistling and shouting Max's name, desperately searching this way and that for any clue to his whereabouts.

"Max…Max!"

CHAPTER 6

Jodie bounced back to her car, excitement flooding every part of her body. Even though she knew her body would be exhausted by the end of the day, she kept going. It had finally happened. She had moved. She was now the proud owner of the cutest little cottage in the cutest little village. Winton Green was her home. And although she had so much to do, nothing could dampen her mood.

Just a few more boxes and she would be done. She had definitely earned herself a strong cup of coffee. And maybe a few biscuits. Bending over the boot of her car, she picked up a box. Something nudged her thigh. Letting out a little shriek of surprise, she dropped the box back in the car and spun around.

"Max!" she exclaimed, recognising the dog beside her. "Where's your owner?" she asked him, looking around. He was nowhere to be seen. "Max, have you run off?" Although he looked quite content sitting there on the pavement with her, she held onto his collar to stop him from running away. There was no name tag on his collar with a phone number to call. "Come on, boy."

Directing him to the front garden, she closed the gate so he couldn't escape. Still, his owner was nowhere to be seen. Walking back to her car, her body tingled with nerves at the prospect of seeing him again. Surely he couldn't be as good-looking as she remembered him. And boy had she remembered him, every day since they met. Which was ridiculous seeing as she didn't even know his name.

"Max!" A shout echoed around her. She looked up from her car again, her heart in her mouth. "Max!" That voice had her hot all over. He rounded the corner near the village shop, running as if in slow motion. Shit. Even at this distance it was easy to see he was just as hot as she'd remembered…if not hotter.

Shaking her head clear, she called out to him, waving her hands in the air to get his attention. "Over here!"

Someone was waving at him across the village green. Hoping that they had spotted Max, Tony jogged over to them.

Realisation dawned on him as he ran closer to the figure. His heart beat faster, and not because of the run. It was the woman from the pub that day. She had come back. It had been months, and he'd lost all hope of seeing her again. Where had she been all this time?

"Hello again." She blushed up at him through those thick lashes when she noticed him looking her up and down. Her dark brown hair was swept up and piled on top of her head and those soft curves of hers were fully visible in black workout leggings and a vest top.

"Hi," he said, a little breathlessly. She walked over to the gate at Ben and Angie's old place. Max sat inside, wagging his tail fiercely, his tongue lolling out to the side. He was happy as

Larry, completely unaware of the havoc he'd caused. Tony breathed a sigh of relief.

"He just came over to my car," she explained.

"How is it that he never leaves my side, unless you're around?" Tony was relieved Max was safe, and equally happy the dog had found his way to her so Tony could see her again. The best wingman you could ask for.

"I'm sorry," she said. "He obviously just loves me more than you." She winked, a twinkle in her green eyes.

"Erm," he murmured under his breath, trying to be serious. A small smile tugged at the corners of his lips. He couldn't help himself, he liked a woman who had a sense of humour. "Thank you for keeping him safe. What are you doing back here?" His eyes locked on hers, and he put his hands into his jean pockets. He was itching to take hold of her. For months now he'd been dreaming of her, dreaming of tangling his hands in her long hair, of pulling her close, bending low and kissing those full lips, pulling a moan of pleasure from her. But now he was too scared to do any of it.

"I'm moving in today." She pointed towards the cottage.

"Oh." Now it was all starting to make sense. "I knew that Ben and Angie were moving, but I didn't realise you were the buyer." Why hadn't he heard about this? He was at the heart of the community after all. John's cheeky smirk that day they first saw her flashed in his mind. Tony would bet money John knew all about it. Mentally shaking himself to stop staring at her in awe, like she might all of a sudden disappear again, he held out his hand to shake hers. "I'm Tony, by the way." He cringed at his formality—he was far too used to being at the pub.

"I'm Jodie." She took his hand, wrapping her delicate fingers around his. Electricity shot up his arm, landing straight in his chest. He searched her eyes for any recognition of the chemistry he felt, but if she felt anything, her eyes weren't giving it away. She was either a very good actress, or she didn't feel it at all. His heart sank.

"Let me help with unpacking your car." He broke their gaze, dropping her hand. "As a thank you for getting Max."

Her eyes lit with surprise. "Oh, you don't have to do that, it's only a bit."

"No, let me help." It was more of an order than a request. He didn't want to leave her just yet. Moving over to the car, he considered two boxes.

Jodie chuckled behind him.

"What?" he asked, turning around, the back of his neck burning.

"Oh, nothing." Her cheeks flushed, just as red as his neck felt.

He prickled. "No seriously, what?" He didn't want her to laugh at him. That was the last thing that he wanted, for her to think he was a joke. When did he start caring so much what someone thought about him?

Shrugging, she said, "It's nothing, I was just thinking about a *Friends* episode."

God, she was cute when she was embarrassed. "What?" he asked, frowning. What was she talking about?

"You know the TV show? *Friends*?" she insisted in dismay. She was obviously a big fan. Who wasn't?

He raised an eyebrow in faux confusion, desperately fighting back his smile to keep up his façade that was getting to her so much. She was even cuter when she was annoyed.

She carried on, her tone growing more desperate. "There's an episode where Joey moves someone into their flat, and chooses the box labelled pillows rather than books. You just reminded me of that." He continued to stare at her, his face unchanging. "Anyway," she said. Moving over to the car to get away from the awkward atmosphere, she picked up one of the boxes.

"I'm joking." He laughed, finally giving in to her anguish and taking the box out of her hands. "I knew exactly what you were talking about, and he had the right idea." Placing the box back in the car, he picked up her pile of powder blue bedding. "Front bedroom, yeah?" he asked, heading to the house.

"No, don't worry, I'll do that later." She tried to take the bundle from him, her cheeks reddening again.

It was so easy to make her blush. Maybe she did have a thing for him too. "I'm helping, so just let me." He winked and dodged past her, through the gate and into the house.

She grabbed the box back out of the car and ran in after him, but he was already up the stairs. "Wait!" she yelled after him.

He stopped and turned back to her. When she joined him on the landing she just stood there, silent, looking at the bedding in his hands, nibbling at her lower lip. He had thought about nibbling that lip way too much these past few months, and a groan almost escaped him. *Get a grip.*

He looked away from that plump lip to her eyes. A hundred questions were etched in her irises. He got it, she felt uncomfortable with him. It was understandable—they were practically strangers—but it still stung. "Look, I know you don't know me from Adam," he said, trying to reassure her.

"Who's Adam?" she asked, her eyebrows drawn together, her voice soft and quiet.

"What?" He scrunched his face up. "It's just a saying meaning you don't know me."

She held her confusion for a heartbeat longer, before a smile erupted from her lips. "I know who Adam is, I'm pulling your leg," she laughed at him.

"Thank God for that." He laughed with her, relieved. "You had me fooled." He rubbed the stubble on his chin. "Payback, I suppose?"

"Yep." She flashed a brilliant smile.

"Well, anyway, I'm just helping out. But if you don't want me in your room, I understand and I can leave it here for you and go and do the rest."

"No, it's fine. I'm just being silly." There was obviously an internal war raging inside of her.

"You aren't being silly," he corrected her. "You're being sensible."

Knowing she had placed her trust in him, he walked through the door and deposited the duvet and pillows on the bed. She stood in the doorway observing him. As much as he would have loved to stay there and joke some more, he didn't want to break her trust. Squeezing back past her as nonchalantly as possible, he headed back down to the car to finish unpacking.

There were only a few items left, so it didn't take them long to lug Jodie's remaining belongings into her home, with Max following them back and forth as they worked. When the last item was unloaded, Tony joined her in the living room where she was trying to move the sofa on her own.

"Let me help," he said again, pushing the sofa with ease. She was obviously an independent woman who was used to doing things herself. Did she really not have anyone who could have helped her out?

"Thanks," she said.

"Is that about right?" he asked, straightening the sofa in the middle of the room a little bit more to get it parallel to the stairs.

"Perfect," she replied, dusting her hands off.

"Why don't you come to The Dog later on?" he asked her, swiping some imaginary fluff off the sofa cushions. "You will have had a long day, and you deserve a bit of a break and a drink to celebrate." He moved the sofa a tiny bit more to the side, not wanting to look in her eyes—her eyes that showed him her every thought. He couldn't remember the last time he'd asked a woman out on a date, and his hands had grown sweaty.

Waiting for her answer for what felt like an eternity, his heart pounded in his chest. She shifted her weight from one foot to the other, her arms crossing in front of her chest. At her continued silence, he searched her eyes. She was scared, nervous. She didn't want a date with him. Not yet, anyway.

He added, "I can introduce you to some locals." He shrugged, as if it were no big deal, yet his heart pounded against his ribcage.

A small smile settled on her lips. "That would be lovely, thank you."

Friend-zoned, already. But it didn't matter. He just wanted to spend time with her. "Great, I'll see you around seven then." He beamed at her and walked out of the front door, calling for Max to follow him before she changed her mind.

"Thanks," she called out after him.

CHAPTER 7

After a little rest on her new sofa that lasted an hour rather than the five minutes she had intended, Jodie managed quite a productive day of unpacking her essentials. She started with her kitchen bits so she could have a cup of coffee and unpack her cool bag with milk, butter and bread to tide her over until tomorrow. She planned a sumptuous feast tonight of beans on toast.

She ate her dinner on the kitchen counter because she still hadn't assembled her dining table, and then ran herself a bath to get ready for meeting Tony. As she watched the bubbles foaming, the smell of jasmine and roses filling the air, she couldn't help but think about him. He'd been on her mind every moment since he left. At first it seemed like he was asking her on a date, but he quickly clarified it was just him being friendly. She couldn't deny that her heart had sunk when he friend-zoned her.

But anyway, what did it really matter? She couldn't afford to be distracted by a man, not with her to-do list stacking up so quickly. She had her home and a business to set up, and adding a relationship to all of that was definitely not a good idea.

A nice long soak in the bath would do her mind and body good, but she didn't have the time. So she cut the bath short in order to get ready.

Sitting on the bedroom floor wiggling her jeans on, because she needed to buy curtains, she made herself a mental to-do list for the next day. Really she should stay at home tonight and get more done around the house, but she desperately wanted to go to the pub. She had earned a little break, right? Besides, she didn't have Tony's number to cancel.

Not wanting to be too dressy, she pulled on a light grey jumper and some tan ankle boots that had a small chunky heel. She was really looking forward to spending some time with Tony. There was something about him that she was drawn to. Not just his heavenly body that surely had abs to die for under his shirt, but also his deep chocolate-brown eyes and the way they creased at the sides when he laughed, and how caring he seemed. But there was something else… something she just couldn't put her finger on.

Unable to find the right bag as they were all still packed, she put her phone and bank card in her back pocket and picked up a book that she was reading, just in case she had to wait for a bit for Tony to show up. Straightening her wavy hair down once more with her palms and applying a little bit of lip gloss, she gave herself one last look in the mirror. There, she had tried hard to look like she hadn't tried at all.

She walked across the green, the pub lit up like a beacon calling her in. The sun was starting to sink in the sky and the clouds were darkening, ready for night to arrive. Now spring had settled in, there was no need for a coat. Which was nice, seeing as that was also in a box in her spare room.

When she opened the door to the pub, Tony was immediately recognisable, talking with some other men, Max by his side. Just the sight of him was enough to take her breath away. He hadn't spotted her yet, and there was no way she had the confidence to just walk up to him, so she went straight to the bar where John stood waiting.

"Jodie," he greeted her and pushed half a pint of cider towards her with a questioning gaze. "Or…" he said, and plonked a glass Coke bottle next to it.

She laughed. "I'm not driving tonight and I happen to quite like cider." She grabbed the glass and took a sip of the cool amber liquid. John put the Coke back into the fridge.

"How'd the move go?" he asked.

She loved that she already felt like a regular. "Good, thanks. Lots to do still, but I'm getting there." She pulled out her card from her back pocket to pay.

John shook his head at her. "Already paid for."

She stared at him, confused. Shrugging his shoulders, he walked away to serve another customer.

A cold, wet nose nudged her hand. She didn't even need to check to know it was her faithful companion. "Hello, boy," she said to him, looking around the bar. Tony was still standing where he was before, but staring intently at her while the other men talked around him. He gave a little wave and a slight smile. He must have bought her drink for her. She beamed back at him and raised her glass in thanks then took another sip. He raised his glass back. God, he was sexy, his hand stuffed in the pocket of his dark jeans, his hair swept back like he had just run his hands through it.

She took a seat at the side of the room, putting her book on the table, happy to wait for Tony to be finished before he introduced her to the locals. Max stayed by her side as she knew he would. Sinking back into the soft armchair, she exhaled heavily, the tension in her muscles ebbing away as peace and tranquillity returned. Winton Green was her home now, this pub was her local, and soon enough she'd know everyone here, she was sure of it.

Allowing herself a minute to sit and be in the moment, she looked around her, feeling completely at ease. Tony had gone back to talking so she picked up her book. Thankfully she had brought it along, otherwise she wouldn't know what to do with herself.

CHAPTER 8

Tony was desperately trying to get away from the conversation and get to Jodie without being rude, but the guys kept jabbering on.

A little while later, he managed it. He picked up some new drinks for Jodie and himself from John, whose smirk lit up the whole pub, and headed to Jodie. At last. She sat reading a book, and didn't notice him appear by her side.

"What are you reading?" His voice jolted her out of the book and into reality.

"Oh," she said, flustered, shutting it. "Just a business book." She took her drink from him and he settled himself in the armchair opposite.

"I'm sorry for not getting over here sooner. Men do talk a lot of old rubbish." He chuckled nervously and looked down at his pint. A lady shouldn't be left drinking alone in a pub, especially when she'd been invited there. It was not a good way to start this 'non-date'.

"It's fine," she told him. "I had Max and my book. I was quite entertained."

He smiled across at her, appreciating her easy nature, and

43

their eyes locked. "Thanks for the drink," she muttered, gazing deep into his eyes.

"Is cider okay? I can get you something else if you prefer?" He made to stand up.

"I love cider!" she exclaimed, to stop him from picking her glass up and returning to the bar. "I mean, not that I drink a lot, but it's what I would have chosen." A pink blush spread across her cheeks. He liked it when she blushed—the pink highlighted her perfectly smooth skin.

"So." He steered the conversation in a different direction. "A book about business?" He leant back, crossing one arm over his body, and put the other hand up to his stubbled chin. He felt awkward around her, aware of his every movement, every word.

"Yep, I'm setting up my own business and my friend sent it to me."

"What business?" he asked, observing her intently. She was perched on the edge of the chair, her hands between her thighs, her thumbs fidgeting together. She shifted, seeming uncomfortable in his gaze. He had to stop being so intense.

"An interior design business for domestic properties," she responded coolly. Sitting back in the chair and wiggling to get comfortable, she crossed her legs, her hands gripping the armrests. She looked like a Bond villain. An incredibly hot Bond villain. She was just as flustered as he was—he smiled to himself—and uncomfortable sitting there in front of him.

Trying to put her at ease, he smiled at her. "What were you doing before?" It was part of his job to get to know his customers, but most of his locals were men, and he knew all about them. Getting to know a woman—a woman he couldn't stop thinking about—was completely new to him.

"Living and working in London for a building contractor." She switched her seating position again, this time keeping one hand on the armrest and bringing the other one over her body to rest on the curve of her hip.

He managed to keep his chuckle to himself, clearly seeing the internal war raging inside her. She was trying to be nonchalant, but it wasn't working and yet again she was stuck in an awkward position and still not comfortable. "That's a big difference." He couldn't help but let his smile escape. She fancied him and he had never felt happier.

"Yep, it was time for a change. There were redundancies on the cards so I decided to take it and move here and start my own business." Her tone was getting snappier. She was probably fed up with being interviewed. But he'd been left so long wondering about her that he just wanted to know everything.

"That was very brave of you." He took a sip of his drink, his hand surprisingly steady when his heart was racing as hard as it was.

"Or stupid." She looked down at her hands twisting, now in her lap.

"No. Brave," he corrected her. She looked up at him, her eyes shimmering at his compliment. "It's one of the most difficult but rewarding things you can do."

With that she relaxed into the chair, seeming to feel more at ease. She cared what he said. She cared what he thought.

"It's something I always wanted to do, but never had the guts to try. Yet now, it all just seems to click."

"Do you have any experience with design?" he asked.

"I have a degree and have done a few projects over the years for family and friends. Everywhere I go, I get taken in by design or people's possessions and how they've used their home or belongings. I like to sit and observe how a place functions and is used, how its personality comes out, and I can visualise how to improve a space. Design is just a part of me now." Passion spilled out of her unchecked. Her blush returned. "Sorry," she said.

"Why are you apologising?" he asked, not wanting her to feel self-conscious. When she had spoken her eyes had twinkled with delight. "What do you notice about this place then?" He wanted to see the sparkle back.

She looked around intently. "I love a space that knows itself. This is the hub of the community. From the outside it ties itself to all the other cottages around the green; they are one together. Yet it has its own personality, its own quirks." She was lost in her own little world. "It's obviously been done out to mimic the ongoing trend of industrial cottage vibes. But the mix of textures is inherently this building. It's what it would have been since its creation. The old wooden beams, all rugged, are perfect in their imperfections. The unapologetic fireplace stands its ground. Just think how many people have stood or sat around that fireplace, nursing their sorrows in bad times or raising a toast in good. This pub is a character all of its own," she finished, her eyes full of wonder.

"I've never heard anyone describe a building like that before." He was completely captivated. "You didn't say what you would change in the decor though?" He considered her some more, steepling his fingers under his nose.

"That's because I don't need to," she said confidently, edging forward in her seat, that cheeky grin returning from earlier in the day. "I don't impose my thoughts and personality on a place, I allow the building to speak for itself."

The corner of his lip curled up in a smile as he stared at her. "I think you'll be very successful," he told her, nodding. This girl had talent and passion. Maybe she could help him with this place—it needed a spruce up. And then he could spend more time with her.

"Thank you." The rosy patches on her cheeks darkened some more as she took another sip of her drink.

"You don't take compliments very well."

She seemed to fumble around for a response, before settling on a simple, "No."

"Do you have any pictures of what you've done? I'd love to see them."

Her energy felt lighter and happier, as if they had broken some kind of invisible barrier. She took her phone out of her back pocket and leant across the table. He met her halfway so they could view the pictures together. Her perfume tickled his nose. If he wanted to, he could reach out and tuck her chestnut-brown hair behind her ear. But no, that would be leading her on. This wasn't a 'thing'. This was just being friendly.

She went through the before and after shots, pointing out a few details to him. He let her talk, enjoying seeing her happy and at ease with him, and being this close to her.

"I'm going to get some part-time work," she finished up. "Well, that's the plan anyway."

"Why?"

She sat back in her chair again. "Just to make sure my bills are covered while I'm setting up. I don't know how long it will take me to get clients."

He nodded in agreement. "That's sensible."

"You're a man of very few words."

"Yep," he replied, smiling. "Drink?"

She nodded and he practically jumped from the seat and headed back to the bar. It was his job to be a man of very few words—customers didn't want to know his problems or achievements. They came here to moan or to celebrate theirs, and he just had to nod along.

"Stop being so intense, man." John patted him on the shoulder after depositing their drinks on the bar. "You'll scare her away." The smirk had gone from his friend's face, replaced by sincerity.

John was right—he should stop treating her like a customer. When he returned to their table, he said, "You must be exhausted from today, after all the moving?" As he handed her the drink their fingers touched for the briefest moment, making his heart beat faster.

"Yes, a bit." She stifled a yawn, apologising. She had settled back in her chair, her cheek resting on her knuckles, as if she could have fallen asleep right there.

"Did you have dinner?" he asked, a little ray of hope appearing that maybe he could take her through to the restaurant and they could eat together.

"Beans on toast," she replied, wrinkling her nose up in a cute little way. "I'll get some more food tomorrow, along with putting up my dining table." She chuckled, yawning again.

"I can put it up for you if you like?" Anything to just spend more time with her.

He had to stop himself from shaking his head. What was he doing? Why was he trying to spend more time with her? This wasn't about to go anywhere. It couldn't go anywhere. He didn't want a relationship. And yet on the other hand, he was trying to spend more time with this woman.

"No. It's fine, it won't take me long."

Along with not taking compliments very well, she obviously didn't like accepting help.

They talked for a while longer about Jodie's plans for her cottage, the life she'd left behind in London and how she had always longed to live in the countryside. Tony drank in every flutter of her eyelashes, every time she nibbled on her lip. She was mesmerising.

"I think I need to make a move," she said to him a short while later.

"Okay," he mumbled, not wanting her to go, but for the past half hour she had been yawning almost non-stop.

"It's been a long day and I have lots to get done tomorrow too."

"Right…of course." He composed himself. "Shall I walk you home?" Just a few more minutes with her, that's all he needed.

"No. It's only across the road. I'm used to London, I'm sure I'll be fine," she chuckled.

"Okay." That was it—she had batted away all his chances to spend more time with her. He didn't know when he'd see her next.

"I'll see you around then, I suppose." She gathered her book and phone, and stood. "Thanks for helping me move, and the drinks."

He still didn't say anything.

She added, "I'll get them next time."

Over his dead body would she. "Not on my watch you won't." He smiled at her. At least she wanted a next time. Keeping his head down to try and avoid everyone's stares, he walked her out into the fresh night air. "Thanks for tonight," he said, hovering over her.

She stood still for a moment, a statue staring up at him, her eyes searching his. Was she trying to read him as easily as he could read her?

He wanted to kiss her, to lose himself in those lips. Tangle his hands in her hair. Make her weak at the knees. But something stopped him. "I'll see you around."

She flinched, stepping back from him. *Shit.* She had wanted that kiss as much as he had. "Yeah, see you around." She bent down to Max and kissed him on the head. "Thanks for looking after me, boy," she whispered to him, and his tail wagged. Why couldn't he be Max?

They watched her walk away, Tony taken by the sway of her hips and Max whimpering beside him.

"I know, Max. I fucked up."

CHAPTER 9

Jodie woke the next morning, groggy from the exhaustion of moving and the cider she had drunk with Tony. She let out a little sigh. She really hadn't wanted to leave him the night before, but she would have fallen asleep in the chair if she hadn't. And then there was that strange moment where she thought he was going to kiss her, but he hadn't. Even now, her body still yearned for him.

Lying on her side, she stared out of the window into the bright blue sky, the silence of Winton Green surrounding her. Yesterday had been a good day, even though she hadn't stopped, what with all the last-minute packing, moving and then unpacking. As she wiggled in bed getting comfortable, her muscles pulled from all the lifting she'd done.

Hoping that caffeine would wake her up a bit, she got up and made herself a cup of coffee before retreating back to bed to drink it. That was one thing she was going to miss about London—the instant coffee from nearby shops. Specifically her favourite one by work. But that was it. That was all she'd miss.

The twinkling music of her phone sounded, pulling her

out of her daydreams. 'Mum' popped up on her screen. Exactly who she needed—it was like she had a sixth sense.

"Morning, Mum."

"Morning, darling. How was your first night?"

"Good. I slept well, but I'm still exhausted. I have so much to do, but I just can't get out of bed yet," she confessed.

"Just give yourself a lazy hour and then get on with a list of things to do. But keep taking regular breaks, otherwise you'll make yourself ill," Sandra advised.

She was right, she always was. With that Jodie sank further down into her bed and pulled the duvet up.

Her mum said, "So what did you get up to last night?"

"I went over to the pub. A local man came by and helped me unload my car and invited me over to meet the locals."

"How lovely. Did you meet lots of people?"

"Well, no actually. We just ended up sitting and talking the whole evening." Jodie could practically hear her mother's eyebrows rise. "Not like that," she added quickly, before Sandra could say anything.

"I wasn't going to say anything," Sandra replied, feigning ignorance.

"It was just nice to sit, have a drink and relax."

"Well, I'm glad you did. Being your own boss can be extremely taxing, you have to do your best to make sure you have a good work-life balance."

"I will do, Mum."

"Okay, well I'll leave you to it. I'm here if you need me. Love you lots."

"Love you too." She settled in bed for an hour more.

After eventually leaving the safety of her bed, she stormed around the house unpacking, organising and creating an almighty to-do list. She even managed to put together her dining table by herself, although it was a lot harder than she had anticipated. Maybe she should have taken Tony's offer up after all.

Her mum texted her during the day, reminding her she should get out of the house—fresh air would do her good. Following her mum's advice, she pulled on her shoes and shut the door on her new little home and all the items on her to-do list. She hadn't visited the local shop yet, and if it was stocked up with the essentials she hoped, then she would at least be sorted till she could get out to do a proper food shop.

Pushing open the door to the shop, she was delighted when a bell twinkled overhead. Although it was small, it was very well organised. It had two rows containing—from what she could see—the majority of items you would ever want. Chocolates, crisps, biscuits, toiletries, medicine. And right at the back, there was a fridge tucked to the side for milk, butter and a small selection of alcohol. This was exactly what she had been hoping for, a treasure trove.

She circled the shop, picking up bits and bobs. She even spotted a bulletin board. There were no job adverts though. So she went up to the counter packed with chewing gum and sweets to pay.

"Hi," she said to the little old man behind the counter.

"Hello," he replied, ringing up her items. "You must be the lady who moved into Ben and Angie's?"

"Yes." She beamed back at him. "I'm Jodie."

"Arnold. Pleasure to meet you. Is this everything for you?"

"Yes, thank you. I was checking the noticeboard you have up," she said, although he had probably followed her every movement in the shop. "Do you get any jobs posted on there?"

"Sometimes," he replied, still putting the items through. "What are you looking for? I'll listen out for you and let you know."

Could being part of a community get any better?

"Anything part-time really. I'm setting up my own business, you see, and just want something to tide me over."

"I see," he said, handing her a carrier bag. "Well, I'll listen out. A few people come in here who have their own businesses, so I'll ask them if they have anything going that might help you." He smiled at her, with genuine kindness for someone he didn't even know.

"Thank you so much, that's really nice of you," she replied. "See you soon." She waved at him as she left the shop, vowing to visit there regularly to support his business.

Upon letting herself into the cottage, she noticed two cards on the floor. The first was from Kelsie.

To my bestest friend.
Congratulations on your move!
We are so proud of you and know you will be happy there.
Cannot wait to come and visit.
Love you lots.
Kelsie and co.

Kelsie had always been so sentimental and reliable. Jodie quickly texted her to thank her for the card.

The next one didn't have a stamp on. Puzzled, she opened it up.

Jodie,
Congratulations on your new home.
We hope you will be very happy here.
From Tony and Max.

There was an outline of Max's pawprint on the card and a little 'x' under Tony's name. How thoughtful. Although she must admit she was a bit gutted to have missed them. She placed her two cards on top of her mantelpiece, and the living room instantly felt more like home.

Suddenly feeling full of energy, she settled down to make her plan of all the bits she needed to do for her new business. First on her list was making sure she had a little office space, even if it was a small bit of floor space for now in her spare room. And then she went about setting up her social media pages.

She seemed to walk on air for the rest of the day—everything seemed so easy and fun. Was it the fresh air that had invigorated her, or could it just have been that card sitting on her mantelpiece with the little doggy print in it?

That night she slept fitfully, tossing and turning. She couldn't understand it. She'd slept so well the night before. But maybe that was from the exhaustion of moving and the cider she had drunk at the pub? Being in the cottage, she couldn't help but feel alone. She hadn't ever thought about it before, but living in London all her life, she had been surrounded by people. And now she wasn't. It was just her. The dark green outside was distracting. In her flat in London, everything was lit up like a Christmas tree and the traffic buzzed below her, no matter what time of night it was. Only now, when it was gone, did she realise how used to the noise she was, how she had needed the hustle and bustle to sleep. Now there was nothing.

No one.

Anywhere.

CHAPTER 10

Pushing through the trees and branches, careful to not get whacked in the face, Tony made his way back from the stream with Max...again.

They had been visiting the same spot every day for weeks now. Every time, Tony sat on the rock, the surface smooth and cold, forcing his mind to concentrate on setting up a B&B, but it always went back to Jodie.

They hadn't spoken since she walked away from the pub. When he dropped a card off for her yesterday, his heart had raced as he knocked on the door. Just like a schoolkid knocking for a girl he fancied. But she hadn't been home and he and Max had retreated, their tails between their legs. And now he had no idea when he would see her again.

Max trotted off in front of him, the woodland path thinning and making way for the main field that would take them back to the village. Bright sunshine rained down on them, blinding Tony momentarily.

His eyes adjusted to the light, and then he spotted something. Max had run off to a figure in the distance. His heart swelled. Jodie. Walking towards them, paying no attention whatsoever, her eyes down, arms crossed.

God, she was beautiful.

"Hi," he called out, and her head jolted up before a sweet smile spread across her lips. "What are you doing here?"

She scrunched her face up in a cute little wrinkle and replied, "I needed to get out."

"You alright?" he asked, standing in front of her, hooking his thumbs in the loops of his jeans. How had he managed a whole day without seeing her?

"Yeah," she brushed him off, bending down to give Max attention, avoiding his gaze.

"Jodie?" he asked softly, forcing her to look up at him.

The green of her eyes turned darker and tears welled in them, her bottom lip juddering in the smallest movement. But he caught it. He caught everything when it came to her.

Taking a deep breath, she looked back down at Max. "I just needed fresh air…it's tough, you know?"

"I know," he replied, grabbing her hand and pulling her up. His heart broke for her. Wrapping his arms around her body, he laid his hand on her head and cradled her against his chest. His heart pounded, beating against her face. She wrapped her arms around him and held on for a second, taking all of his support. With her glorious body pressed against his, her tension seemed to ebb away. She was surely a little slice of heaven.

"Thank you," she finally whispered, tipping her head back to look at him. "I needed that."

"Anytime," he whispered back, staring intently into her eyes as they broke apart. He instantly missed her body. "Are you walking back with us?" he asked cheerily, trying to hide his obvious reaction to her.

"Yes, please. I thought I could find my way back, but now I'm not so sure."

They walked a little while together, watching Max in front of them sniffing at the grass and exploring all the smells of the wild. Wrapping her arms around herself as they walked together, she said, "Thanks for my card."

"That's alright. How are you settling in?"

"I love it, but it's the hardest thing I've ever done." She sighed.

"That's to be expected though," he offered, glad she was opening up to him.

"Yes, probably. I just didn't realise. I was more acclimated to London than I thought."

"What do you mean?" He furrowed his brow at her.

"It's so quiet here and I do love it. But as much as I find that peaceful in the day, during the night it's disconcerting."

He nodded.

"I'm just not sleeping," she blurted out. "And I get grumpy when I don't sleep." She gave a small laugh.

"I can't imagine that."

"I just have to get used to it, I suppose."

"Lack of sleep makes everything seem harder. Can you sleep during the day?"

"I have too much to do." She sighed again. "I have a whole house to unpack, a business to set up, bills to pay."

"You're stressed." Tony could feel it radiating from her. That easy nature, their joking with each other, had disappeared.

She bristled, her jaw clenching together. Whoa, she really *was* grumpy when she was tired. "Yes." She shook her head and carried on walking, one step in front of him. "I'm going to try and find a part-time job while the business is setting up, but if I can't, I might have to go into full-time employment. But that will mean I won't have as much time to work on the business, so it'll take longer to get up and running. Then what's the point at all?" she ranted, barely taking a breath.

"Whoa!" He stopped her on the path, holding his hands up, and made her take a deep breath to stop her from talking and having a panic attack. "One thing at a time, okay?" He held her arms and stared deep into her eyes. She breathed out slowly, her shoulders dropping, and nodded.

Once she was finally calmer, if only a little bit, he offered her a glimmer of hope. "There's a waitressing job going at The Dog."

"What?" She wet her lips. "That would be perfect. Why didn't I think of that?"

"Because you're too emotionally attached to your situation. Sometimes it takes someone else to show you the way." He let her arms go. This would be perfect—he'd get to see her more and help her out in the same turn.

"Who should I give my CV to?" she asked, immediately zoning out, not paying any further attention to his answer. Probably trying to remember where her CV was.

He smiled down at her. "Me." God, he wished he could kiss her, bring her back to right here and right now. He wished he could run his hands over her soft curves and make her moan against his lips.

She glanced up at him. She obviously hadn't paid attention. "Sorry." She blushed, the pretty pink shade covering her cheeks once again. "I was trying to think where my CV would be saved. Who should I give it to?"

"Me," he repeated, raising his eyebrows in a bemused manner.

"What do you mean?" She scrunched her face up.

Before he smoothed out those lovely wrinkles on her forehead, he carried on. "You should give your CV to me, seeing as I own the pub." He grinned. Her face morphed from confused to a look of dread as she realised her mistake. "Did you seriously not know that?" He chuckled.

"Why didn't you tell me?" she bit at him, running her hands through her hair.

"I thought it was obvious. Why would I spend all my time there?"

"I don't know." She waved her hands in the air and brought them down to slap her sides. "I thought maybe you liked your drink," she admitted quietly.

"Seriously?" He raised his eyebrows at her. "You thought I was an alcoholic?" He wasn't easily offended, but something about her not even considering he could own the pub, the fact she thought it was more likely that he had a drinking problem, made his blood simmer. "It didn't occur to you that it was my pub?" It shouldn't irritate him, he shouldn't be upset. But it did. And he was.

"I didn't really think about it," she replied quickly. "Anyway, you could have told me, but you're such a closed book, I know nothing about you." She crossed her arms.

He scoffed. Attack was the best form of defence, and she was trying to place the blame solely at his feet. He looked down at the grass and scuffed the ground up a bit, thinking, weighing up his next words carefully.

"Would you like the job at The Dog?" he asked her calmly. Calmer than he felt. But he wanted her to feel secure, to be able to achieve her dreams. And covering a few shifts at the pub could do that for her. "You don't have to give me a CV," he added. "It's a perk of being the boss, I can do what I like." Looking up at her, he gave a wink. He didn't want to fight with her. It was much better when they were playful.

"Yes, please," she replied, equally measured as he had been. Then she added quickly, "I have had some waitre—"

He cut her off with a quick shake of the head, gritting his jaw in frustration. Why couldn't she just let it be? Realise that this was his way of apologising for being a closed book to her when she was an open book to him.

But she carried on, "I thought you would want to kn—"

"Stop!" he told her firmly. "I don't need to know. The job is yours. Let's go."

CHAPTER 11

Tony's back was hard as stone as Jodie followed him back to the village across fields and pathways. She kept a few steps behind him, letting him have his space. Max was off in the distance, blissfully unaware of the awkwardness between them.

Why was he so guarded with her? It was obvious that she had offended him. She hadn't meant to—of course she didn't think he had a drinking problem. She hadn't thought at all. And that was the problem.

She pulled her cardigan closer around her body, shielding herself from the chilly air sweeping across the field. They had been getting on quite well. She was extremely attracted to him —her body seemed to spring into action whenever he was near. Certain parts of her body buzzed around him. Or even at the thought of him. Certain private parts that she wished would stop buzzing at that very moment.

But more than that attraction, which surely would fade when she was used to those chocolate-coloured eyes that drank her in, or those hands that she willed would touch her. She honestly believed they could be friends. He was the only person she had met so far in Winton Green who could be considered anything close to being a friend. But maybe not. Surely it wasn't right to get so irritated with one another when they hardly knew each other?

"We can cut through here," he told her, indicating a little woodland trail. He led the way through the narrow, overgrown path. Trees and brambles snatched at her clothes. Tony weaved this way and that and she followed blindly, still thinking.

What did she really know about him? Well, now she knew he owned The Dog…and that he had a dog. She made a mental list. He could be quite sarcastic…he was caring. She knew how her body craved his touch when she was around him. When he hugged her, he shared enough strength to make up for weeks of no sleep. When he stared into her eyes, it was like he was reading her thoughts. When he smiled at her, it was like her whole heart had been filled with sunshine and rainbows and butterflies landing on spring flowers.

God, Jodie, get a grip.

But other than that—the things he made her feel—she knew so little of him. And she wanted to know so much more.

The toe of her boot knocked against something hard and unmoving on the ground and she was propelled forward, hitting that strong, rock-hard back with a thud. Gripping onto his t-shirt for dear life, her legs caught up with her and she was able to stand and right herself. He whipped around, holding onto her arms, steadying her.

"What happened?" His grip tightened on her forearms, his eyebrows knitted together.

"I must have tripped on something," she said, searching the ground for what had sent her flying. "It must have been a root. Sorry, I wasn't looking where I was going."

"Are you hurt?" he asked, his head bent low, his intense eyes searching her body for any sign of injury.

Her body instantly responded to his hungry gaze, warming all over. "N-no," she stuttered. It had only been a little trip, but her heart thumped in her chest. Maybe that had something to do with how close Tony was—just in reach to nudge his nose with hers, to kiss those lips of his.

"God." He sighed with relief. "You scared the life out of me." He gave a little laugh, the frown on his forehead melting away.

"Sorry," she whispered. *Kiss me, please just kiss me.*

"Come here, you wally." He pulled her into a hug, again resting his hand on her head and keeping her close to his chest. The tension had left his body, his strong arms encasing her. All she could hear was his pounding heartbeat, all she could smell was him and all she felt was comfort and support. Wrapping her arms around him, she held on for a second, taking all his support and storing it as strength. How quickly they could go from bickering like children to this. Whatever *this* was.

Finally breaking away, Tony led her along the path, setting a slower pace this time and keeping an eye on her as they trudged through the brambles. It was so nice to have someone look out for her. His protection was like a warm blanket wrapped around her shoulders.

"So we've sorted out your part-time job," he called back to her. "What else are you worrying about?"

"The house and the business…and sleeping," she added.

"Well, hopefully this walk will give you a better night's sleep," he said. "All businesses take time. All you can do at the beginning is work hard and keep motivated to continue. When I took the pub on, it wasn't like it is today. It was run-down and hardly any of the locals visited it. It was a sinking ship. I spent all the hours I could doing it up in the day, and all night dreaming up new ways to get the locals interested in the place again. Once they started coming more regularly, the work still wasn't over. I wanted it to appeal to the wider community and make it a place people would come to visit from afar. I had to set up the restaurant from scratch. Now look at it—years down the line, it's pretty successful, better than I imagined it could be. But I still have to keep working."

She froze, her mouth open, drinking in every word he spoke.

"What?" he asked, stopping when he realised she wasn't walking with him anymore.

"I was just making the most of actually listening to you. That's the most you've ever said to me."

"No it's not," he scoffed, and turned to keep walking.

"Yes it is," she called after him. "Thank you." Maybe there was something between them?

"Whatever." He didn't look back, but she didn't need to see his face to know he was smirking.

"Can you come in for your induction tomorrow at four?" he asked when they reached her cottage. "That gives the guys some time after the lunchtime rush and before the dinner guests arrive. Then you could work in the evening? It shouldn't be too busy on a Tuesday night."

"Of course," she replied, grabbing her keys from her pocket. "What should I wear?"

"All black. And comfortable," he clarified, breaking her from her thoughts.

"Thanks, Tony." She stared up at him, anticipation bubbling in her tummy. He had been a bit of a knight in shining armour since she arrived. "Are you heading back to the pub now?" she asked, not ready for him to leave just yet.

"No. Heading back home."

"Where do you *actually* live?" she asked, intrigued. She might as well make the most of him opening up.

He gave her the same smile he had before he told her he owned the pub. Leaning closer, he pointed for her to see.

"That cottage there," he said softly, so close to her ear that it sent shivers down her spine. Then he pulled back. "Same kind of cottage as yours. Right next to the pub. Not a bad commute, really."

"Really?" she asked. There was so much about Tony that she obviously didn't know. And yet he was her only friend in this new village of hers, and there was so much more she wanted to ask.

"Yes," he replied with another smile. "You can watch me walk in if you want to be sure," he added, already walking backwards along the road. Was he flirting with her?

"I have better things to do with my life, thank you!" she called after him, enjoying his playful side.

"Yeah, right!" he shouted, turning around and walking away with Max.

She could have stood and watched them both go. But that would prove him right, so she forced herself to turn and let herself into her home. She could always watch them from her living room window.

No...that would be creepy.

CHAPTER 12

The next day Jodie arrived at The Dog for her induction five minutes early, with butterflies flying around her belly. It was silly to be so nervous. She knew Tony. She knew John. And everyone here seemed super friendly. But it had been a long time since she worked in a new place and had the daunting task of impressing the boss and settling in with her colleagues. And she'd be lying to herself if she didn't admit that those little butterflies—well, maybe some of them—had something to do with the possibility of seeing Tony again.

She had picked out her all-black outfit following his request—just a t-shirt, jeans and ballet pumps. Her wavy hair was tied back, so she didn't get any of it in the customers' food, and her make-up was simple—a little bit of eyeliner and a dash of light pink lipstick. Just the thought of seeing Tony again brought a natural pink to her cheeks, so there wasn't any need for blusher.

Taking a deep, calming breath, she opened the door to the pub. It was the quietest she had seen it, the calm before the storm when the evening customers came in. Her heart dropped slightly when she couldn't spot Tony. But John, as always, stood vigil at the bar, smiling warmly at her.

"Here for your induction?" he asked.

She nodded in response.

"Before I grab Micha, Jodie, this is my sister Sophie. Sophie, this is Jodie." He motioned to a pretty young woman with long blonde hair who was sitting at the bar.

"Nice to meet you, Jodie. I've heard all about you."

John turned to Jodie and rolled his eyes. "Not from me," he explained, "I'm no gossip. Anyway, let me grab Micha for you." He walked to the restaurant area around the back of the pub.

Once he'd disappeared, Sophie turned back to her. "Tony has been telling me all about you."

"Really?" Jodie gulped down a little lump that had formed in her throat. She knew that Tony wasn't hers to get jealous about, but that didn't stop a horrible sick feeling from settling in her stomach.

"Oh, don't worry." Sophie patted her hand. "Tony's like a big brother to me. There's nothing to worry about there."

Before Jodie could say anything else, John returned with a tall, slim woman who held her hand out to shake Jodie's with a warm, welcoming smile on her face. She wore all black too, with a name badge pinned to her t-shirt reading 'Restaurant Manager. Micha.'

"You must be Jodie?" She beamed. "I'm Micha. Let's get you round the back so we can have a quick chat."

Micha showed her the back of house, where Jodie deposited her bag. Micha leant against a table and rested there for a while.

"So Tony said you'll be joining us here for a few shifts?" Her question hung in the air and Jodie tried to not see judgement behind it. She didn't want everyone to think she had got the job just because of knowing Tony, even though that was exactly how she'd got it.

"Yes, if that's okay?" She clasped her forearm in front of her body. "I did some waitressing back in university and just want to get to know the locals and earn a bit of money while I'm setting up my business."

"That's good to know." Micha nodded. "What shifts are you looking to work?" She pulled a notepad and pen out from her back pocket.

"Anytime you need me really." Jodie shrugged, trying to sound breezy. "I don't have any commitments at the moment, so whatever best helps you out."

"Okay." Micha put the pen and pad back into her pocket. "I work out the rota with Tony so I'll let him know, and we can see what's needed and go from there." She slapped her hands on her thighs. "Let me show you around then."

She gave Jodie a tour of the restaurant and a quick demonstration of how the till and ordering system worked. Once they had finished, Micha said, "Let me introduce you to the other guys on this shift before anyone comes in. They should be in by now."

They returned to the back room and Micha introduced Jodie to two others, Hannah and Ryan, before going out for a cigarette.

Hannah looked the same age as Jodie, and was very petite with blonde hair pulled up into a bun. Ryan was a lot younger, probably just out of sixth form. "So Micha has shown you around?" Hannah asked, pinning her name badge to her t-shirt.

"Yep. How long have you two worked here?"

"I've been here for a few years now, and Ryan joined us before Christmas." Hannah spoke on Ryan's behalf, who just nodded in agreement.

"Do you like working here?" Jodie rummaged through her purse to spruce up before their shift.

"Everyone who works here is so friendly. We're our own little family, aren't we Ryan?"

Ryan was barely able to get out his "yeah" before Hannah carried on.

"I mean it is still waitressing at the end of the day; it can be hard work. Most of the regular customers are nice. Some of the out-of-towners can get rude, but you expect that at any place. The team is what makes it different though. Micha and Tony are great bosses."

"That's good to know," Jodie replied, putting her lipstick back in her purse.

"Have you met Tony yet?"

The heat she felt in her cheeks and across her chest was a sure sign she was blushing. "Yes, I have."

Hannah's eyes twinkled and the corners of her lips lifted up at Jodie's reaction. "Hunky, isn't he?" She chuckled. "You'll see him lots around here, so that little crush,"—she gestured her hands all around Jodie's body—"will soon go once you get to know him and see what a great boss he is." She winked at Jodie just as Micha returned to save her.

"Come on then, Jodie, let's head out and finish setting up the tables. Hannah, I've already seated a couple for you."

They all made their way out of the room and went about their individual tasks. Jodie followed Micha around for a while, feeling like a puppy trailing its master. Serving customers was more daunting then she had expected it to be; it had been so long but she knew it would all become second nature. All night long, she kept an eye out for Tony, hoping he would pop his head round to check in on her, but she never saw him.

By the end of her shift, her feet burned and her mind was frazzled. Hopefully she'd be in for a better night's sleep.

Jodie's week passed in a wave of exhaustion. Every muscle hurt from walking the restaurant floor, every bone ached to the core from getting her house sorted, and her brain was numb from working to get her business started.

In between her shifts at The Dog—where she longed to see Tony and was always disappointed if she didn't—she researched software and suppliers, created a portfolio, shared bits on social media and tried to find that first elusive client. Eventually life would be normal—she would have jobs flowing in, her pretty little cottage would be fully unpacked and decorated, and hopefully she wouldn't have to work shifts at The Dog because her business was so successful. But now... everything was hard work. And she just needed sleep. But her body wouldn't even let her do that.

Yesterday she had thrown in the towel and spent all day lounging on the sofa in her pyjamas, snuggled under her favourite blanket, watching *Friends*. She could have been getting on with so much more, like throwing together some mock-up moodboards, or recording all of her expenses and dismal lack of income, or even unpacking the last few boxes in her spare room—but she had to give in.

Today though, was a day for action. Today she would start painting the living room and making it hers. Stamping her mark on the place. And of course documenting it all for social media posts. No one else had to know it was her house that she was working on.

The white work came first, which was mind-numbingly boring, but maybe if she got it done quickly enough she could get some colour on the walls and instantly transform the space. That was the fun bit. What she disliked even more than painting the white work was laying down all the masking tape. She cranked up some music and set about her task.

As she worked her way around every nook and cranny, careful to not spill the paint or splash it up the brick fireplace, her hands ended up covered. She had even managed to get splatters over her clothes and a mysterious spot on her sock, which she had then walked through the living room. Why was there always a splodge of paint you walked through?

Making a start on the bannister, she cursed. Why hadn't she hired someone to do this for her? It was a pain in the arse. Sighing some more, she sat on the floor to continue painting. This would take hours.

Sometime just after lunch, she was lost in the boredom of her task when there was a loud knocking on her front door. Heaving herself up from the floor, her legs stiff from sitting in one position for too long, she put her paintbrush down.

She opened the door to a smiling Tony and the ever-faithful Max, who walked straight in to greet her.

"Hello, boy." She knelt on the floor to give him a cuddle and attention. God, she had missed him this past week. And Tony too of course. She looked up at him. He stood there, smiling down at them both, leaning against her door frame, his arms crossed, showing off his muscles. Hannah was wrong. This little crush of hers wasn't going anywhere.

CHAPTER 13

"Sorry to intrude," Tony said, breaking into Jodie's greeting with Max. He looked around her wreck of a living room, her furniture pulled into the middle, covered in dust sheets, the paint fumes filling his lungs. Little specks of paint littered Jodie's clothes and hair, which she had pulled up in a bun on top of her head. Even with baggy clothes on, her small curves called out to him, just asking to be touched.

This week had been torture. He'd tried to stay away from her, so he didn't get too attached, but he'd yearned for her company every single minute. And it didn't help seeing her at the pub so often. More than once she had caught him gazing at her while she was working, and he had to suddenly pretend he had another place to be.

"You're getting round to painting, I see."

"Yep," she replied, dark circles under her eyes.

She was still tired, and her tiredness made her cranky; he had learnt that the other day. Normally she would have made a witty remark, joked around with him that he wasn't the sharpest knife in the drawer. But not when she was tired. He instantly missed her witty banter.

"Do you want to come in?" she asked, getting back up off the floor and holding the door wider for him to come through. "We can sit in the kitchen. That will be a bit easier." They followed her, Tony attempting to stop Max from walking or wagging his tail in the wet paint. "Would you like a drink?"

"No, I'm fine thanks."

She got a bowl out and filled it with water for Max. He loved how she treated Max, always caring for him, always spoiling him with attention.

"What can I do for you?" she asked, jumping up to sit on the kitchen counter while Tony leant against the sink. Max was slopping water all over the floor.

"You look tired."

She stifled a yawn and shrugged. "I just have a lot going on."

"You're overworking yourself. You'll end up burning out." He frowned at her.

"I had a rest day yesterday."

"But you're still tired."

Shrugging again, she jumped down and started drying the dishes on the draining board, all the while avoiding looking him in the eyes.

"You still can't even rest."

As she went around the kitchen, putting away the dishes, he stared at the back of her head, hoping to somehow get through to her. She ignored him as she moved on to putting the cutlery away. Although she said nothing, there was no hiding that underneath the surface her emotions were bubbling away. Any moment she would break. And it was anyone's guess as to whether she would break down in tears or in anger.

Reaching for her hand, he swung her round to face him, demanding her full attention. She clutched a teaspoon in her hand as if it were her only defence from scrutiny. Why couldn't she just look after herself?

"Jodie!"

As she stared deep into his eyes, her tears started to well. His frustration broke the moment he saw them, and his eyes searched hers for her unspoken words.

"Jodie," he muttered softly. If she wasn't going to look after herself, he would have to. Pulling her towards him, he wrapped her in a hug, her soft body moulded against his. The perfect fit, as if she were made just for him. "Talk to me," he pleaded quietly.

"I just can't sleep," she admitted, tears rolling freely down her face, marking his polo shirt where they fell. "That must sound so pathetic, but I get so grumpy when I'm tired and I feel so lonely. I'm not used to being on my own. I always had my flatmates with me, and then I would always be able to hear neighbours, but now there's noth—"

"Shhh." He cut across her rambling, stopping her from spiralling out of control. "I get it, everything is worse when you can't sleep."

"Every time I lie in that bed and try to sleep, my mind kicks in and I think of all the things on my to-do list that I haven't ticked off yet. Every spare minute I have is either researching, networking or planning. I just can't shut off. I must be missing something. There must be something I haven't thought of yet, or haven't done to get my first client. But no matter what I try, I can't come up with anything else. I know setting up your own business takes time and effort, but it's so bloody hard."

"I get it, Jodie. Sometimes you just want someone to bounce ideas off or even tell you what to do. You'll get there, I know you will." Sweeping her hair away from her face, he whispered to try and calm her, "Go upstairs and get into bed. I'll bring you up a cup of tea, then you can have a nap." It wasn't a suggestion, it was a command. Yet she tried to pull herself out of his embrace and refuse the offer.

"I can't—"

"You can, and you will," he practically growled, letting her go but keeping his eyes fixed on hers. Never before had he wanted to care for anybody, and it wasn't his problem that Jodie wasn't looking after herself. But he couldn't just walk away from her. He wanted to help, to protect her, to make her happy again. What was it about her? "Max and I will stay here and finish painting while you rest. That way you won't be alone." She went to protest again, but before she could even form her first word, he spoke again. "Don't even bother arguing." Taking her shoulders, he turned her firmly in the direction of the door. "Upstairs...now." It wasn't a shout, just a clear, curt sentence that had her following his orders.

He made a cup of tea and found some biscuits that he placed on a plate for her. He'd bet she hadn't eaten in a while either. He knew why she was running herself into the ground. It was so easy to do as a business owner. He understood—he'd had more than his fair share of sleepless nights because of the pub. You either didn't sleep dreaming of all the possibilities and your future, or you didn't sleep because of nightmares about finances or HR issues.

He went up to her bedroom with Max, concentrating on the task of not spilling a single drop of tea. Max immediately jumped on the bed and snuggled up to the other side of her. Jodie stroked him.

"I'm sorry," she mumbled to Tony as he placed her tea on the bedside table. He shot her a questioning look. "This is all just a lot, being here, and everything is new. Maybe I'm not cut out for this?" Her worries escaped her, as well as her tears. Max looked up at her, big droopy eyes full of concern, mimicking Tony's feelings.

"Oh, Jodie," he sighed, his heart breaking for her, as if it somehow affected him too.

He joined her on the bed, his back against the headboard next to her, and wrapped her in another cuddle. She rested her head on his shoulder.

"You just need to sleep," he whispered against her soft hair, and kissed it gently. "Everything will seem better after a sleep...I promise."

CHAPTER 14

Stretching out sleepily, Jodie felt the hard body beneath her, the arm wrapped around her shoulder and the rhythmic rise and fall of Tony's breathing. *Shit.* How on earth had she fallen asleep on him? God. How mortifying. He was her boss. What sort of employee fell asleep on their boss?

"Are you awake?" he whispered softly.

She raised her head and shifted her position so that she was leaning on one arm, and looked up at him through bleary eyes. His hair was swept back, his hand behind his head.

"I can't believe I fell asleep on you," she said with a wince. Lying here, like this, was far too intimate. It should be awkward. But every moment felt glorious, and she couldn't resist relishing every second of it.

He chuckled in response. "Do you feel better?"

She took a minute to mentally evaluate herself. "Yes," she admitted. "That was the best sleep I've had here."

"Good." He pulled her back down to lie on his chest, his eyes closed and a happy, triumphant smile on his face.

So much for worrying about him being her boss. "What's the time?" She stifled a yawn.

He brought his watch up to look. "Five o'clock."

"Five?" she nearly shouted, raising herself up again to look at him.

"Five," he confirmed and brought her back down. Placing his hand with the watch back behind his head, he traced her arm with his thumb. Max yawned next to them, quite content.

"I can't believe I slept for that long." She was worried. "Aren't you meant to be at the pub by now?" She looked up at him, her cheek resting on his chest.

"Yes," he replied calmly, his eyes still closed, a small smile on his face. He looked as content as Max did. Sensing her staring at him needing more of an answer, he finally gave in. "I got Micha to cover for me."

"What?" Jodie asked, shocked. Hannah had told her that either John or Tony were always at the pub, in case of any issues. But John had booked off holiday time and so Tony was meant to be covering for him. They had other bar staff, so it was more just someone there to be the ultimate manager.

He shrugged underneath her. "Micha has been wanting more responsibility. She's been there a long time, and she's trustworthy. She can handle it." Jodie stared at him, trying to digest his words. All the staff at The Dog were trustworthy and good workers, but that didn't mean that Tony relied on them. From her little experience of being there, it was obvious he liked to do a lot of the work himself, even if others could do it. "It's no big deal," he finished up, sensing her unasked questions.

She rested her head back on his chest in defeat. It felt like a big deal.

They lay there for a little while longer, comfortable in each other's silence. Tony continued rubbing her arm. Was this normal to do with a friend? It definitely wasn't normal to do with your boss. And she certainly had never done this with Kelsie before.

He cut across her thoughts. "What do you want for dinner?" he asked softly.

"I haven't even thought about it." In truth, she could just stay there all night and not need any food at all.

"I'll make you something nice." He must have noticed her resistance because he added, "Just let me take care of you. It's one night. What harm can it do?" He squeezed her shoulder.

She gave in. "Okay." They were both stubborn, she had come to realise, and she didn't want to ruin the afternoon with an argument so small.

"Good," he beamed, enjoying his small win. He rolled her over onto her back, his chest almost on hers. "You stay here for a bit and I'll see what you've got." He kissed her forehead softly before jumping up and heading off downstairs with a spring in his step that hadn't been there before.

She smiled as Max jumped off the bed and rushed after him, probably keen to be let out into the garden. She snuggled down in the soft blanket that Tony had so kindly placed on her. The spot next to her was still warm from his body, his masculine scent wrapping around her. One more minute wouldn't hurt. Really, what harm could it do?

Probably a lot, she sighed. And then her heart took a nosedive. She hadn't ever felt this way about anyone...ever.

Before she could relish in her full minute of bliss, she was seized by panic. *Her paintbrushes.* She hadn't tidied them away properly before coming upstairs. She flung the blanket from her and rushed downstairs, making an almighty racket. Tony rushed from the kitchen to see if she was okay.

"The brushes!" she blurted, turning the corner from the stairs, hoping she would be in time before they were ruined.

"I wrapped them in cling film while the kettle boiled," Tony said when she picked up the brushes in bewilderment. "Do you like carbonara?" he asked, walking back into the kitchen.

"Yes," she called after him, shocked he had thought about tidying away for her.

"It won't take me long," he added, heading to where bacon was already frying in the pan. The smell was glorious and had her tummy rumbling.

Sitting down at her little table, she watched him working away, seeming to be quite at home. With his back turned, she was able to admire his strong, broad frame and the way he moved skilfully around the kitchen, not following a recipe but following his instincts. As he cut through the flesh of the chicken, she admired the way his muscles moved. The pan sizzled next to him as he threw in piece after piece.

Tony was lost in his task, and she was lost in him. Hannah had said the crush would subside, but it seemed to be getting worse. Jodie found him infuriating in some ways—he was stubborn and opinionated, she still didn't know a lot about him personally, and probably the most annoying was how transparent she felt around him. He knew exactly what she was thinking, no matter how hard she tried to disguise it.

But with all that, he was also caring and generous, so far her only friend here who she knew she could rely on. And without a doubt, she knew he only wanted the best for her.

As charming and kind as he was, and no matter how much her heart fluttered when he was near, she knew that falling for him was out of the question. She couldn't afford to get sidetracked. She couldn't risk ruining her only true friendship here. This had to be strictly platonic. No more falling asleep on him. She sighed.

As if sensing her burning stare on his back, he turned around, scrutinising her in return. "You alright?" he asked, midway through cutting the last chicken breast. The pan hissed noisily next to him.

"Course," she replied with a friendly smile. *Platonic*.

His eyes searched hers and he looked like he wanted to say

something else, perhaps open up. But as quick as a flash it was gone. Nodding a friendly smile that mirrored hers, he turned back to complete his task. Jodie released the breath she didn't know she'd been holding.

At a loss for what to do with herself and not wanting to get told off for going and painting some more, she joined Max out in the garden and played with him, allowing Tony to finish cooking.

A little while later, while she was busy chasing Max around the garden for the ball he didn't want to drop for her, Tony's frame caught her attention leaning against the back door, he stared at them playing, a small smile on his face. Their eyes met for a few seconds, with neither of them breaking the connection.

"Dinner's ready," he finally called to her and turned to go back inside and sit down at the table.

She walked into the kitchen, feeling a bit flushed and breathing heavier than normal. A large plate of piled-up carbonara greeted her on the table, opposite Tony's. He sat waiting, not yet touching his meal, his elbows on the table and his chin resting on his knuckles. His mouth was slightly covered by a few of his fingers, almost guarding his kissable, full lips.

"Thanks," she said in an overly cheery manner, trying to cover up the fact that she'd been staring at him. "You can start," she encouraged him, as she took her seat.

Not uttering a single word, he started to eat in silence.

"This looks lovely," she added, feeling awkward and wanting to fill the void of conversation. She twirled some spaghetti around her fork. Still he said nothing. Great, he was shutting down again.

"So," she punctured the silence again. "You never told me why you came round?"

He said nothing. Jodie was just about to kick his shin in frustration when he eventually broke his silence.

"I just wanted to ask you about covering a shift," he replied, looking down at his food. She hadn't known him long, but his shifting eyes and his leg bouncing up and down under the table were all she needed. He was lying.

"Really?" She hated lying. Placing her fork down on her plate, she raised her eyebrow at him, staring at him even though he was trying to avoid her gaze.

He didn't reply.

She took a calming breath before continuing. "Normally Micha just texts me." She left the statement hanging in the air. What she really wanted to say was, "Bullshit. You're a crap liar."

"I just offered to pop in as I was going past." He still didn't meet her gaze, his incessant knee twitching getting faster.

She considered him for a moment. After another calming breath she said, "Okay."

Her short response was enough to get him to look up at her in alarm, his eyes wide, those luscious lips slightly parted. Probably at the realisation she knew he was lying.

Wanting his guilt to eat away at him, she continued on. "Do you want a drink?" she asked in a pointedly pleasant fashion. She rose from the table and scooted past his chair.

"Water, please," he replied, scraping his chair closer to the table to let her pass.

She filled up his glass of water and leant over him to place it on the table next to him. As she leant she placed her hand on his broad back for support, and felt the tension in his rock-hard muscles beneath her fingers. Once she'd filled her glass, she returned to her chair. She ate two more small bites of carbonara before placing her fork down.

The silence screamed in the room.

Tony had almost finished his meal, but Jodie's wasn't even

half eaten. "Do you not like it?" He gazed at her, a frown creating a deep v between his eyebrows.

"I'm not very hungry," she responded curtly.

He placed his fork down as well and sat back with a sigh. "Okay," he exclaimed, raising his hands up. "You win."

"Win what?" She fluttered her eyelashes at him innocently.

"You know what." *Sore loser.* "I didn't come round to ask about covering a shift. I came round to talk about your interior design skills."

Jodie was knocked off kilter—she wasn't expecting that. "What do you mean?"

"I came round to ask to be your first client."

"Oh…" She was stunned. She *really* wasn't expecting that. Thoughts ran wild in her mind.

"But then I saw how tired you were looking, and you're not looking after yourself at all. You've piled too much on your plate and you aren't even taking the basic steps to feed and water yourself. You've been covering loads of shifts at The Dog—how could I ask even more of you?"

"Tony." Jodie cut across him softly. Even though she enjoyed seeing him rambling on—just like she'd done herself so many times before—she'd never seen him this way, this vulnerable. "I would love that."

"But how can I?" he said.

"Tony." She stared him straight in the eye, silencing him. "I would *love* that." She felt warm and fuzzy all over, like hope was soaring through her veins. "This is what's needed to set up a company, you know that," she said to him in a much softer tone. "How many sleepless nights did you have? How many times did you overwork yourself?"

"But that was different," he argued.

"Why?"

"I don't know, it just is."

"It isn't, and you know it." She smirked at him, liking being

83

in control and seeing him uncomfortable. Twirling another bit of spaghetti in celebration, she took a careful bite, never breaking eye contact.

He clenched his jaw, trying to hold back his smile, but there was no mistaking it was there. "You're annoying."

"Ditto." She could've burst out laughing at the sulky look on his face. "So," she added, trying to make the atmosphere lighter. "What would you like me to work on?"

He picked up his fork to continue eating. "My house." Back to the short answers and being guarded again. She noticed he didn't refer to it as his home.

She tried to pry more information from him. "Which room?"

"The living room and bedroom to start."

She tried not to let the shock settle on her face that he wanted her to design both rooms. Her heart pulsed. "Okay. Obviously I'll need to come round to view the house, to see what it's currently like and talk about what you're looking for. But what time scale are you hoping for?"

"As soon as possible really. You can come round whenever you like," he offered up, finally finishing his dinner.

She thought about her schedule. Virtually everything could be pushed around to accommodate this work. Sure, she had some shifts at The Dog booked in, but she might be able to take a couple of days off. "What about tomorrow lunchtime?" she offered.

"Perfect."

"Obviously I won't charge you anything. This is the perfect way to document my process for future clients and build my portfolio. Thanks, Tony." This was just the thing she needed to get her going.

"I *will* be paying you." he pushed his chair back and grabbed both of their plates to tidy up.

"Tony, you're doing me a favour," she said, trying to stay in charge of the conversation. She walked round to where he was scraping the remaining bits of her dinner into the bin.

"No," he said, looking into her eyes. "You're doing *me* a favour." She opened her mouth to argue some more. "End of, Jodie." He turned his back to do the washing up.

And just like that, they were back to normal. Tony in control and them bickering like kids. She dried the dishes next to him, using the silence to contemplate their strange relationship. Was it normal to fight as much as they did? No, probably not. Yet it never made her think badly of him or hate spending time with him. It was just them, both stubborn and wanting to be in control. Her mum had always said that fighting showed you cared.

"Thanks." She nudged him with her shoulder, giving in.

He looked at her, his hands covered in soft, soapy suds, a little smile on his face.

"I'm looking forward to it," he admitted, his dark brown eyes almost twinkling.

"Me too," she breathed. This was going to be dangerous. But she just couldn't resist.

CHAPTER 15

After they finished cleaning up, Tony showed Jodie to the living room, uncovered one of her chairs and insisted that she sit down while he finished painting the bannister. Max quickly snuggled next to her, the two looking so peaceful together. She had tried to tell him no, that she didn't need to rest anymore, but she gave in quickly. It was obvious that she was exhausted, even though they'd had the most wonderful, inappropriate nap known to man. Forcing her to sit and rest was overbearing, sure, but she needed it.

"I still don't know a lot about you," she called out to him.

He was sitting on the stairs, paint brush in hand, concentrating on the detailing. Max rested his head on her lap, sleeping yet again. The two of them had become best friends so quickly.

"What do you want to know?" He wasn't a naturally open person. Part of owning his own pub meant that you knew more about others, and that suited him to the ground.

She contemplated for a moment. "How long have you been here?"

"About five years now. I bought the pub and house having

saved up a lot of the money for it, and I had a vision for how I wanted the pub to be. It's been a struggle, but it's what I've always wanted."

She smiled at him. Was it really that easy to get her to smile at him with that twinkle in her eye? "What did you do before the pub?"

"I've always been in hospitality." He carried on painting as he talked. "I've worked in pubs and clubs and hotels, but I knew I wanted to be my own boss and in the heart of a community. So I worked tirelessly, saved up and followed my dream."

"What about family?" she asked.

He looked up at her, considering his answer, and she blushed slightly under his gaze. "What about family?" He wasn't sure he really wanted to talk about family. Ever. To anyone.

"Well, did you have a happy childhood?" She fiddled with a cushion.

He saw the concern surface on her face, probably worried that she'd hit a tetchy subject. And she had, but not for any bad reason, just that he wasn't close to his parents. When he was a kid, it hadn't been unusual for them to sit together at dinner in silence, or for him to spend hours in his room playing on his own. He hadn't looked back when he left for university, only visiting in the holidays, and as soon as he'd graduated he moved out permanently. Now his parents spent a lot of time travelling and he didn't see or speak to them much. The pub and Max were his family.

"Yep." He continued painting. "I'm an only child. Mum and Dad worked lots and were quite successful. I didn't want for anything."

She took time to consider his answer. Reading between the lines, no doubt.

"Where are they now?" she asked.

"They still live in the house I grew up in, that's in Surrey. But they spend a lot of time abroad now, travelling. And John and his sister Sophie are like my family down here."

"Yes, I met Sophie and she said you were like a brother to her."

He looked up in surprise. "When did you meet her?"

"At my induction. John introduced us."

"They're pretty great, really. John and I always have a laugh, and Sophie would be happy if it weren't for her crappy boyfriend."

Jodie smiled at him. "Overprotective much?"

"You wouldn't say that if you met the bloke. Soph could do so much better than him. She just can't see it."

"And how long will you keep telling her that before you realise she won't ever listen, and that she needs to make up her own mind about her relationship?"

Tony stopped painting. He and John had never given Sophie any space to contemplate her relationship. They both knew full well that Scott was a good-for-nothing excuse of a man. And neither of them could understand why she was still with him after all these years.

Jodie rolled her eyes. "Have you ever thought that maybe whenever you two tell her she shouldn't be with him, you're pushing her to stay? Let her be, let her make her own decisions in life. And just be there for her when she needs you."

"Huh…I hadn't thought about that."

"I can tell." Jodie shook her head at him. "What about Max?" she asked. On hearing his name, Max raised his head, nudging her for a scratch.

"I always wanted a dog when I was growing up, so at the first opportunity I got Max. He's usually always stuck by my side, but it appears he prefers your company to mine." He laughed.

"Well, who wouldn't?"

"Oi, Miss," Tony wagged the paint brush. "Remember who's painting your stairs."

Jodie laughed and went back to stroking Max, while Tony painted in silence. This was all completely new to him, this feeling of companionship. He hadn't ever wanted to spend so much time with someone as he did Jodie. And this little... infatuation with her...surely it would pass.

Probably by the time she was done redesigning his house, he would remember why he didn't date. Spending all that time with her would remind him what hard work women could be, remind him that all relationships ended in unhappiness.

But a little feeling, deep in the pit of his stomach, didn't believe that at all.

～

Jodie hadn't slept well again. But hey, that wasn't news anymore. This was different, though. A mixture of excitement and anticipation. This is what she had been waiting for. Her first client.

Okay, yes, it happened to be Tony—her friend and now boss, who was probably just 'pity-hiring' her—but right now she'd take anything.

The whole morning, she had paced up and down, clock watching. She had even reorganised her bag five times. And finally, unable to resist anymore, she turned up to Tony's house ten minutes early. She just couldn't wait to see him and Max again.

Her friend, she reminded herself, shaking her head. But she had never been this excited to see Kelsie before. She shoved the thought away. She couldn't afford to be distracted today.

Knocking on the door, her heart thumping through her

89

chest, she waited for him to answer. She had yet to be inside Tony's house, although since she found out this was where he lived, every time she walked to and from work she tried to have a peek inside without it being too obvious.

The door opened and Max's nose immediately appeared to greet her, as did Tony's smile. His eyes drank her in, the colour of melted chocolate.

"You're very punctual." There was a cheeky glint in his eye. He was dressed casually in jeans, bare feet and a black, tight-fitting t-shirt. He looked heavenly.

Shit. Not even a minute in and she was finding it hard to think only friendly thoughts. How was she going to survive this one? "I wanted to make a good first impression," she replied, giving Max a stroke.

"You already did that."

She could feel the heat rising up her cheeks. Was he flirting with her?

"Come in." He opened the door wider and watched as she walked past.

The layout of his cottage was the same as hers, with stairs in the living room directly in front of the door, the kitchen at the back, and two bedrooms and a bathroom upstairs. She shut her eyes and stood still for a second as Tony ushered Max back in and closed the door. Breathing in the house's smell, she could tell he'd had a bacon sandwich for breakfast, but she could also smell him. His woody, leathery aftershave, his fresh laundry powder, his smell that was just Tony.

The house was as silent as hers—he had no music or TV on and she could just hear Max and Tony's footsteps and breathing. The house was just that. A house. Not a home. Although she could smell and hear Tony, she couldn't feel him in the cottage. It could have been a hotel room.

Opening her eyes, she surveyed the front room. The floors were a practical dark wood, perfect for Max, but had no rugs to soften its harshness. The walls were painted magnolia, one of her most hated colours and now so out of date. A dark leather, two-seater sofa sat in the middle of the room, along with an armchair that Max now settled himself in, creating a walkway to the kitchen. The beautiful, original fireplace was covered by a large TV and sleek white TV cabinet, and there were modular storage cabinets either side of the fireplace.

She walked to the covered fireplace to view the room from different angles. Tony stood watching her, his arms crossed, leaning against the bannister, giving her the time she needed to review the space. There were a few mismatched picture frames on the partially covered mantelpiece. From a brief glance, she could see that the majority were pictures of Max, but some were of family members, she presumed. These were the only personal possessions she could see in the room. The only things that identified this house as belonging to Tony. Yet she was sure they had all been birthday or Christmas presents. The frames didn't seem like Tony and she couldn't see him taking time to buy frames and print out pictures to fill them.

She brought her eyes up to him. She'd been aware of his presence and of him intently watching her, but had absorbed all of the room before looking at him.

"Would you like a drink?" he asked, the glint still apparent in his eyes.

"Water would be lovely. I brought some lunch too." She held up the shopping bag she was holding that had fresh bread, cheese and meat in it. He came and took it from her grasp, their fingers touching for the briefest second. Yet that small brush of his skin sent tingles up her arm.

He went to the kitchen to deposit the bag and get her a drink. She followed him to survey the room. Although she wouldn't be touching it, she wanted to get a feel for the whole house and how he lived in it. A little two-seater table was nestled in the nook under the stairs and the countertops were clear of clutter.

"How do you want to do this?" he asked over his shoulder.

"I think we should just sit in the living room and talk for a bit and then do the same upstairs," she suggested.

"Alright. Then we can have lunch."

She nodded in agreement and they sat down in the living room, squeezed together on the small sofa. Tony lounged more casually than her, one knee resting on the cushion as he faced her with his arm resting along the back of the sofa. His large frame was too big for this sofa—that would be the first thing to go. She pulled out her notebook and pens.

"So," she began. "I think the best way to do this is to discuss how you currently use and feel about the space, and then how you want to use and feel about it once it's been decorated. We can go over the sort of things you like and dislike. I'll make notes and maybe some initial sketches. Then I'll put it all together and produce a plan for you."

"I thought you were going to let the place speak for itself. Like you said about the pub."

"No," she corrected him. "That's a passive place that many people use in different ways and has a true identity all of its own. But this place is your home. Your identity should be shown here, in harmony with the house."

He nodded in understanding.

"So how do you currently use the space?" She poised her pen, ready to make notes.

"I'm hardly here," he replied.

She waited silently, her eyes on him.

"I suppose when I am,"—he continued and Jodie felt a sense of relief—"me and Max might sit down for a bit, maybe watch the telly or a film. But I mainly use the house to eat and sleep," he admitted.

"Why do you think that is?" she asked him.

"I've been so busy with work and getting the pub where it needs to be. I don't have time to laze around."

She smirked at the irony that he didn't practice what he preached.

He must have realised the irony too as he added, "Yes, alright. And I don't like being here."

"Why?" She felt sad for him that he had no comfortable place other than the pub, where he was on show. On all the shifts she'd had so far where Tony was there, not once had she seen him on his own, someone was always by his side, demanding his attention.

"It's just empty and quiet," he shrugged. "And cold."

She knew he wasn't referring to the heating, but to the way the house felt. It wasn't his home. It was his shelter at best. A place to rest his head, wash and eat before his next shift began.

"That's because this place doesn't reflect you." In that moment, she knew Tony needed some comfort and encouragement that she could change that. But she refrained from taking his hand. She didn't trust her body to not react to his touch. And they were just friends, after all. "Nothing about this place, so far, speaks of you. It could be a hotel. Your home should make you feel welcomed and comforted, a place you want to come back to and recharge."

"I can't see that ever being the case." He looked around the room, despondent.

"It can," she reassured him. "Trust me."

He nodded, and she was lost in his eyes.

Then, remembering her purpose, she refocused on her notebook. "So how do you want to use the space?"

He shrugged, so she continued.

"Do you want a sanctuary or a home theatre? Do you want to entertain or have a family?" Her cheeks heated up. Maybe she had gone too personal with that last suggestion. Maybe she'd asked that subconsciously to get a feel for where he was in life. Gulping, she stared at her paper, ready to write his response, pretending she wasn't on the edge of her seat to hear his answer.

"Just a place for me and Max to rest, I think." He eyed Max, sleeping on his armchair.

Jodie understood. There was no place for anyone else. She understood, but her shoulders still dropped. "Is Max attached to that chair, or will another one be just as good?" she asked, trying to keep the conversation light and cover the stab to her heart.

"Any will do, I think."

She nodded and wrote some notes. "What's your budget?"

"There isn't one."

She raised an eyebrow at him. "There's always a budget."

"If you can make this space feel how you described, then there's no budget."

She considered him. Maybe, if he was to let someone else into his life, he wouldn't need an interior designer to create a home for him.

"Well, I think there's a lot I can do here. I would repaint obviously, move the furniture around." She rose from the sofa to indicate how she saw the space. "I'd get a corner sofa along this kitchen wall and an armchair for Max on the opposite side. Do you know if your fire still works?"

Tony sat still, watching her as she walked and talked. "Should do."

"Well, I can get someone round to dust the flue and check its safety. I need to get mine done anyway. We have to uncover it—a man in the countryside with a working fire should not have a TV in front of it. Imagine cosy winter nights in with a roaring fire." Her mind wandered away from her with romantic scenes.

"I don't have cosy nights in," he told her, his voice raw.

"Well, maybe that's because you can't get to your fire."

There was nothing better than a cup of hot chocolate, a snuggly blanket and a roaring fire. How romantic. An evening in, lounging back with the one you loved. Heat rose through her, as if the fire was already lit. "You're missing out," she added quietly.

"On what?"

He surely saw her blushing, surely read her thoughts and knew exactly what she had been thinking of. It made her cheeks burn even more, knowing she was so transparent to him.

"Cosy winter nights in," she said again shyly, fully aware he could read her like an open book. "Max would love it."

"He wouldn't be the only one." His voice rumbled low, his eyes darkening, catching and holding her gaze.

"No," Jodie whispered. Needing to snap herself out of his hypnotic trance, she took a clearing breath and carried on past the chemistry bubbling between them. She was here for business, pure and simple. "So we'd have to move the TV into this corner, and make it less of a focal point." She gestured to show him where it would sit.

"I'm all on board." He nodded.

"Good. We can discuss colours and furniture later on." In control again, not wanting to be tempted by him, she remained standing.

"Will you be bringing painters in?"

"I normally would, but I haven't found any I'd want to work with yet, so for now I'll do all of the painting."

He clenched his jaw.

"What?" she asked, sitting down on the edge of the sofa cushion.

"You're overworking yourself already."

She scoffed. "Really? After your comment about not having time to laze around?" She didn't give him any time to respond. "Let's have a look at your room."

He led her upstairs, Max following behind them dutifully. Tony's scent intensified as she reached the top of the stairs. What even was that smell? She couldn't put her finger on it. But it was just Tony. Just delicious.

This man fascinated her too much. She was playing a dangerous game. *Do not let yourself get distracted.*

He opened the door and stepped to the side to let her view the space like she had done in the living room. The stark whiteness of the bedroom walls shocked her senses as she entered. The bright white walls were matched by crisp white bed linen, dark navy curtains hung at the window, and underneath sat a little dog bed for Max, who was now nestled inside it.

The bed sat in the same position as Jodie's, although she doubted it would fit any other way. Opposite he had an exposed hanging rail in place of a wardrobe, and although everything was hung very neatly, it made the room feel cluttered. The exposed floorboards again had no rug to break up the expanse of wood. The space felt clinical rather than welcoming and relaxing.

Next to his bed sat one bedside table, on the side furthest from the door. There was no room for anyone else. Not even space for someone to stay the night and put a glass of water at their side of the bed.

"I can see which side you sleep on," she half joked, pointing to the table that had her mesmerised.

He wrinkled his brow, unsure what she was getting at.

"You'd let a woman sleep nearest the door?" She raised a teasing eyebrow. Why was she trying to find out more information about him? She had decided they were only friends. Why did she need to know about his sleeping habits?

She was only making the observation to find out more about him and whether he would ever be open to her. To them. And he wasn't. So move on, Jodie. She turned and went to look out one of the windows.

"I don't have women here," he growled. His low voice reverberated through her. Was he annoyed or aroused?

"Hard to believe," she said, looking out over the green and to her cottage across the way. Keenly aware of his eyes boring into the back of her head, she didn't dare move, needing the time to gather herself again. *Keep it professional.*

Turning back round to face him, she plastered a smile on her face.

"Do you want to sit?" he asked, his growl having disappeared. He motioned at the bed, and her smile vanished as quickly as it appeared. He sat at the end of the bed, nearest the door, while she sat on 'his side' nearest the window. She felt uneasy in his intimate space.

Professional, she reminded herself, before asking, "So how do you currently use the space?"

He laughed out loud.

"I'm not asking for sordid details about your sex life!" she exclaimed across his laughter, heat rising from her chest and up her face, more in annoyance than embarrassment.

He calmed his laughter slightly. "I told you, I don't have women here." His eyes glinted with laughter still.

"Then why would you laugh and assume that's what I was asking?" She was frustrated with him—she despised being laughed at.

He shrugged. "It's just an awkward question to be asked."

"It's exactly the same question I asked downstairs," she retorted. She had meticulously laid out her client journey with the questions she would ask and the experience they would receive. Him questioning even a slight part of that journey made her feel like she was an imposter, that she didn't know what she was doing.

"We weren't sitting on a bed downstairs." He smouldered across at her, and her breath hitched at his intensity.

"Well…" She stumbled for words. "I wouldn't ask anything like that." To avoid looking into his eyes any more, she doodled a little star on her notepad.

"You've already mentioned cosy nights in and having women in my bed, so who knows what other information you want to coax from me. You seem to enjoy questioning me." He flicked something off his thigh.

She defended herself. "I was merely making a light-hearted point about making a woman sleep nearest the door. And cosy nights to me mean pyjamas and hot chocolate."

"You could have fooled me," he whispered, but she cut across him.

"And I've only asked you a few questions—which you could have refused to answer, I might add—to glean a bit of knowledge of who you are. We're meant to be friends."

"Are we?" he asked, his eyes locked on hers.

"Well, you're my boss and now my client," she fumbled, ignoring his lust-filled eyes. Did he mean to flirt with her? Probably not…he was probably just lost in the moment. Friendship with the opposite sex could get complicated. Well, that's what she'd found out from movies—she didn't have any experience in the matter. "So, Tony, how do you use this space, apart from sleeping, having sex or masturbating?" She poised her pen at the ready, staring holes through her notepad. *Shit.* Had she really just asked that? *Please ground, just swallow me up now.* That is what you got when you let someone crawl underneath your skin.

He spluttered with surprise. She forced herself to not look up at him, her pen still on its point on the paper to make notes. The ink dot it leaked was like a black hole she wanted to throw herself into.

"I sleep here."

She wanted to hurtle across the bed at his infuriating form and pummel him. Why couldn't he ever just let her in?

He carried on. "I wake up early and take Max for a walk, then I get changed here after a shower and leave for the day. When I come back, I change and go to sleep." He paused as she wrote. "Do you want to know what jammies I wear?" he asked with cheekiness laced in his voice.

She ignored his remark. "Do you read, or listen to music, or watch anything?" She would get through this debacle if it killed her.

"No. I'm normally too tired." The smirk in his voice had gone. He must have finally realised he'd angered her.

"How do you want to use the space?" she asked, still looking down.

He shifted on the bed. "I suppose I want to come here to feel relaxed and comfortable."

"So," she said, jumping up off the infernal bed that had her hot and clammy all over. "We can't do too much to the layout due to the size. You do, however, need a wardrobe. That will do wonders to make the space feel decluttered. And you must have two bedside cabinets." She paced round the room, aware he was following her every move. She couldn't look at him on the bed. "From there, I've already come up with a few ideas on design. I would reiterate the design concept throughout the house, so it feels succinct and well thought out. Option one, 'Minimalist Masculine'. White walls with black and dark grey colours. Option two, 'City Masculine'. Dark colours with sleek, clean lines. Option three, 'Rough Masculine'. Textures with wood, brick and fur, light greys and browns, dimly lit and a bed that looks better messy." She finally looked at him again, her heart beating hard in her chest. "Do you want to see some examples?" She made to get her phone out of her back pocket. She'd stayed up late researching some themes for today.

He shook his head. "Rough Masculine," he confirmed. His voice had turned gravelly, his eyes narrowed and he was holding onto the bedspread with white knuckles.

"Thought so." She knew that would appeal to him, but right now, he seemed to be actually smouldering. She gulped, trying to compose herself. "You already have the wooden floor, are you happy for me to install faux brick on this back wall, or better yet, expose the brick behind?" she asked, walking past him and the bed. "And we'll need to change your bed for a metal frame one." She looked back over to him where he was gawping at her, for want of a better word.

He gave a brief nod of agreement, looking ready to pounce on her, lust filling his now black eyes.

"Shall we eat some lunch then?" she asked, to break the intensity. He looked as if he wanted to throw her on the bed and devour her. But she wasn't on the menu. Couldn't be on the menu. They were just friends.

CHAPTER 16

While Tony unpacked their lunch, Jodie sat at the table, scribbling away and sketching and grabbing sample images to present to him. She was cute, lost in her world. Her passion for design poured from her as she created. This truly seemed to be her calling in life. She was completely oblivious to him, which allowed him to stare at her freely. How did she get more beautiful every time he saw her?

He shook himself. He was getting into dangerous territory. A long time ago, he'd made a promise to himself that he wouldn't end up like his mum and dad, in a relationship void of love, laughter or happiness. Relationships were doomed to fail. But Jodie...well, she was getting under his skin.

He placed lunch in front of her. "Eat," he ordered, otherwise he knew that she wouldn't.

Without looking up, she reached to one side and pulled her plate towards her.

He returned with his own lunch and sat down on the chair next to her. "Jodie?" he said softly when realising she had yet to take a bite. "That can wait, concentrate on eating."

"I'm almost there," she replied, still scribbling away. He

huffed his disapproval, but a minute later she looked up at him with a small smile. "See!" she exclaimed. "I'm done."

He looked at the sheets of paper in front of her. She had remembered every little detail, and more. The new armchair just for Max, the rug in front of the fireplace, his new sofa that he could actually fit on. And then in his room the metal frame bed against the brick wall. He could have groaned at all the dirty thoughts running through his mind. Jodie lying naked in front of the fireplace. Jodie bound to his new bed. He cleared his throat. But failed to clear his mind.

The details didn't really concern him. He'd lived in an empty box all these years, after all. Anything would be an improvement. And if even a little bit of what she said she could achieve actually came to fruition, this would be worth every penny. But what had got him started on this project had only been one thing. Jodie. If he could help her get on her feet, break that barrier of getting her first client, he would have achieved his goal. "Great. When can you start?"

She swallowed her bite of sandwich. "Hang on, don't you want to see the detailed plans? I can get them to you within a few days."

He shook his head. "No need for all that. I trust you. Do what you think is best." Getting up from the table, he deposited his empty plate by the sink.

"But I would normally draw the plan on the computer and offer samples of colours, fabrics and furniture, and price it all. Then arrange a time scale of work. Then you could agree to it."

"I don't need to see all of that. You know what you're doing, and I won't disagree with any of it. Here." He dug into his back pocket and pulled out his wallet, then walked towards her with his credit card held out. "Use my card to buy everything and then tell me how much to pay you for your time." He retreated back to the kitchen counter, leaning against the side, ready for a fight.

She just held the card, her gaze holding his, her eyes wide. "But—"

"When can you start?"

"I...I don't know," she replied, now staring at the card in her hands.

"Well, start as soon as you can. And obviously when your energy allows you to."

"But why the rush?" she asked, searching his eyes.

He knew what she saw there. Desire. Desire to feel her hair between his fingers, desire to run his tongue along her body, desire to kiss her. But most of all, desire to just spend time with her.

Shit, and now desire between his legs. Shrugging, he turned around to clear the crumbs from the side, hiding from her knowing gaze. "I just want this house to feel like you said it could," he muttered, busying himself. It was true, he wanted this house to feel like his home. Max's home. And that nagging feeling still hadn't settled—it was telling him he needed something more, something different. Maybe this would suffice.

"Are you sure?" she croaked.

His head shot around at her question. "Jodie," he said. Why did she always question everything as if she weren't good enough? It killed him to think she didn't know her worth. He took a deep breath before saying, "I'm sure."

She rose from the chair and walked to him. He squared his shoulders, clenching his jaw, ready for the ensuing argument.

With determination on her face, she stood on her tiptoes and wrapped her arms around his neck, embracing him in a sincere hug. "Thank you, Tony," she whispered into his ear.

He circled his arms around her curvy waist and snuggled his face into that sensitive little crook of her neck, making sure that he kept his hips from connecting to hers. He didn't need to show how she got to him. As they stood there, entwined together, he memorised every part of her, unable to move even if he wanted to.

"Thank *you*, Jodie." His wispy words made her shiver beneath him.

"I can start tomorrow," she whispered back, still not letting go of their embrace.

"Good." He squeezed her soft body gently.

Max jumped up at them, breaking their intensity, one paw resting on Jodie's arm and another on Tony. He stared between them both and they laughed, breaking further apart. Tony bent down to stroke him and give him attention.

"I think someone's a bit jealous," he muttered, rubbing Max's head and ears and giving him kisses. "Don't worry mate, we still love you." He carried on scruffing him up.

Then he looked up at Jodie. She was in her own little world, staring at them both, her eyes glazed over. Daydreaming. "Jodie?" he murmured gently, bringing her back to the world.

"Sorry?" she replied, apparently with no idea what he'd said.

"You look lost."

As he stood up beside her again, she muttered incoherently. He smirked. She'd felt it too. That undeniable connection they had.

Grasping her hand that she had resting on the sink, he brought it around his waist, enveloping her in another embrace. The tension in her body eased away as she once again settled against his chest, breathing him in. As if that was where she belonged.

He wrapped his hands around her body, resting one on her shoulder blade, the other on the small of her back. Then he leaned casually back on the counter, her body pressed against his. He kissed the top of her head tenderly before laying his cheek on the same spot.

They stood there for a few minutes, just being.

Just friends…right?

≈

Tony was waiting for Jodie to arrive the next morning to start on his living room. He had moved the furniture away from the walls into the middle of the room to avoid her doing any heavy lifting.

The comfort he'd felt from her yesterday still shocked him. He'd never felt like that with a woman. She was his friend, he had come to realise. Someone he wanted to see and speak to every day. But now, he was also her only source of income. *Shit*, what with the waitressing job and now being her first client, he was getting himself into a sticky situation. Without even realising it, Jodie had invaded his life. Every aspect of his life. How was he meant to resist her now?

She was due to turn up any minute, and knowing without a shadow of a doubt that she would arrive without having had breakfast, he started making a bacon sandwich for them both. She had wound herself into his life and he wasn't sure he would ever be able to untangle her from it. And did he even want to?

Her knock on the front door brought him out of his thoughts. She smiled up at him when he opened the door, all cute with her hair tied back and slouchy clothes on. Her jeans were paint splattered and her top had a deep v-neck cut which showed off the tops of her breasts. Yes, she did get even more beautiful every time he saw her.

"Morning." He took the heavy paint pot and bags from her and ushered her in. He noticed her looking at him, drinking him in, and his muscles twitched underneath his white t-shirt.

His body responded to the sight of her licking her lips, her tongue leaving a delicious wet trail in its wake. He was glad he had his hands full of bags and paint, otherwise he would have had his hands full of her.

She stopped staring to greet Max, who was sniffing her eagerly for attention. "I'm going to make a start on the white work today," she told him over her shoulder. She seemed to be aware that he was staring just as intently at her as she had at him. "Then I can get the walls painted, and then it will be a case of finding the right carpenter for the units and getting a sofa. I already made a start last night on sourcing a lot of the finishing touches."

"Okay," he said, still standing by the door, paint pot in hand. "I'm helping you out today."

She spun around to look at him. "Shouldn't you be working?"

"I will be...on my home."

She continued looking at him, probably trying to read him like he could read her.

He shrugged and added, "It's too much to do on your own." He could see that she wanted more of an explanation from him, but she wasn't about to get one. She wrinkled her nose up, about to argue, but he said, "You get started and I'll finish making us bacon sandwiches." He went into the kitchen to stop her from saying anything.

He busied himself with making the sandwiches, but his mind was solely on the woman in the other room. *Snap out of it, Tony.* What on earth was happening to him?

He finished making their breakfast and took their plates out to the living room.

"Thanks." She took the plate he handed her and the cup of coffee. "I need this, I was up late last night."

"Did you need me to come sleep with you again?" He raised an eyebrow, unable to hide his grin.

She choked on a bit of sandwich and he had to pat her on the back. Her eyes watered as she looked back at him. "No, I was up buying bits for this place."

"Ah, so I'm going to have a big credit card bill this month?" He couldn't deny he was a little bit disappointed.

"Hey, you did say there was no budget. And you did say you wanted it started as soon as possible." She sipped at her drink, finally back to normal after her coughing fit.

"I didn't expect you to start spending so quickly." He winked, letting her know he wasn't serious in the slightest.

"Well I think I've found some good options for sofas and ones that won't take six weeks to be delivered. And of course it's all the finishing touches and trinkets that will make it, so I have to start getting them."

"You're not overworking yourself, are you?"

"No." She tore off a bit of her bacon and handed it to Max who was waiting patiently next to her.

He was used to her now, used to telling when she was attempting to hide something. "Jodie...what time did you go to sleep?"

She screwed her nose up. "Two in the morning."

He groaned and took her empty plate.

"But I got loads done," she said, "and it's one of the best bits. I loved it and had so much fun."

"I'll take your word for it."

"Did you want to see the sofas I found? It's a pretty important item, I don't want you to not like it. And we should probably go and try them out and see what you prefer."

"I trust you, you know that. You're the expert."

"Yes, but you can't hate the sofa. It's not like some little trinket that you could hide. You have to love it."

"What's a trinket?"

"Just a little knick-knack." She laughed at him. "You have to think the sofa is comfortable. I think we should go sofa shopping. Even if it is just to test out the ones I found."

He had been about to tell her to just get whatever one she thought was best, but the prospect of spending more time with her—even if it was hours shopping—couldn't be passed up.

"Okay, I'm in."

She clapped her hands and then downed the last dregs of her coffee before handing him the empty cup. "Let's get to it then." And she turned to start painting.

They had been at it for a while, listening to the radio he had put on for them, when she said, "You're making a regular habit of skiving off work."

"Only for you, it seems." He bent his head to paint. *Shit.* Maybe this wasn't a good idea, being here with her all day.

"You know you don't have to be here and supervise me," she said. "Unless you don't trust me in your house?"

"I don't trust you to look after yourself and stop to eat or rest," he told her matter-of-factly. That was partly the reason, but he'd be kidding himself if he didn't admit he was excited at spending the whole day with her.

"I would," she insisted.

He shot her a look. "Did you eat anything this morning before coming over?" he asked, one eyebrow raised. She carried on painting, her cheeks blushing. He could see it spreading to the top of her chest too. He stifled a groan and forced his eyes back to the painting. "Exactly." He knew he was right.

"I'm capable enough," she said quietly.

"I know you are," he said softly, staring down at her with comfort and support. He had no doubt she could look after herself, to do anything that she wanted to do. But she seemed to always put herself last on the list. Was it so bad if he put her on the top of his list? "I just like taking care of you." His admission tumbled out of him before he could stop it. "Does that annoy you?" he asked her, softly again but braced for her reply.

She shook her head. "No, it's nice to be cared for." She carried on painting. After a short moment, she said, "We bicker a lot, don't we?"

He nodded in agreement. "I wouldn't have it any other way." He continued to paint as well, keeping himself busy, just like she was doing. This bloody painting must be working like one of those therapy tactics. Where you talk more without meaning to just because you weren't paying full attention. He had never been so open with his feelings.

She blushed at his sentiment. "Me neither."

CHAPTER 17

"Alright John?" Jodie asked when she arrived at The Dog a week later. "Is Tony around?" Today was the day she had been counting down to. Sofa shopping. Sure, it was probably ridiculous for her to be so excited about a piece of furniture that didn't belong to her, but it was a piece of the puzzle for Tony's home—a huge piece—and they needed to get it right.

"How's it going, Jodie? He's down in the cellar. Go and shout for him. Knowing him, he could be down there for ages."

Jodie hesitated. She hadn't been down in the cellar before and it would probably be creepy. But John had already turned to pour some more drinks and so she had no choice but to be brave. She walked behind the bar into the back room where there was a little dishwasher, spare glasses and drinks, and the cellar door was open. Max was sleeping peacefully in the corner.

Taking a deep breath, she descended the steep stairs, cursing her choice of footwear. High heeled boots were not the best thing. When she was at the bottom she called into the gloom, "Tony?"

The space was larger than she had expected, with different spaces separated by brick archways. Although there were lights on, they were dim and she had no idea where he could be.

"Tony?" she called again. There was some rustling in one of the rooms to the side, so she made her way towards it.

She ducked her head under the low arch and there Tony was, surveying and moving the large beer barrels. He was nodding away, and then she spotted his earphones. With his back to her, he had no idea she was down here with him, so she took a few steps forward and tapped him on the shoulder.

He jumped at her touch and quickly turned, taking out his earphones. "Sorry, Jodie, I didn't hear you come down. Is it that time already?" He swiped the tumbling hair from his eyes.

"Yeah, but we can postpone if you have stuff to do?"

"Nah, I could be down here all day organising all this stuff. Waste of time really. John says I do it because it makes me feel important." Tony pocketed his earphones and looked around him laughing.

"Well, we all know that's not true. This place needs you. It wouldn't be the same without you."

He looked back at her, a small smile tugging on his lips. "I mean, if you want to drop that into conversation with John anytime, then feel free."

They laughed together, everything so easy between them. This past week, she had either spent her time at his house finishing the painting, or working shifts here. And for most of those shifts, Tony was also around. She couldn't deny she loved spending time with him, even if they weren't really talking or doing a lot. It just felt natural. Maybe they could do this being friends thing; it sure did seem to be going well at the moment.

"I haven't been down here before," she said, looking around at the cellar, with its brick walls and low arches. It was strangely quiet, even though they were right underneath the bar. "It's different from what I expected."

"Have you not? Well, it's not much to look at. I'm sure you would prefer to get shopping?"

Tony walked past her and ducked his head first through the arch she had come through. When it was her turn, he held his hand for her to take as she bowed her head, and made sure she didn't bang it. "Steady now," he said, making sure she had cleared the arch.

When she stood back up, she was closer to Tony than expected, his hand still gripping hers tightly, his eyes capturing hers with a dark stare. She sucked in a breath, feeling hot all over, despite the coldness of the cellar. He inched closer to her, their bodies almost touching. If she just leaned forward, her body could connect with his, she would feel that hard chest of his, be able to look up into his eyes and maybe lean forward to kiss him.

His other hand—the one that wasn't holding hers— reached up to her cheek, where his thumb wiped her skin. "You had an eyelash." His voice was rough and raw, and it seemed to reverberate right through her. He kept swiping at her cheek, her need deepening in her belly every time he stroked it.

"Thanks," she whispered.

His thumb stopped moving, but his palm stayed cupping her cheek, his fingers crushing against her neck, sending delicious tingles around her body.

Without saying another word, he pulled her forward ever so slightly, his body moving to close the gap between them. She could almost feel him against her, could almost taste his lips. She had been waiting so long for this moment, so long to finally kiss him. She fluttered her eyes closed. Screw being friends. She needed him, and she was tired of waiting.

"Tony?" John called from the top of the steps.

She immediately opened her eyes and Tony suddenly disappeared, his hand leaving her cheek, his other wrenching from her grasp. She had to control the whimper that wanted to escape.

"Yeah, mate?" Tony stood at the bottom of the steps looking up. How had he managed to get there so quickly? Her brain was hardly working from their kiss, let alone her body.

"Did you want me to keep Max here while you two go shopping? He might prefer it to being in the house on his own."

"Sounds great. Thanks, John."

"No problem. Is Jodie still down there with you?"

Then Tony finally looked at her, his eyes saying something she couldn't begin to understand. He took a deep breath, "Yeah, she is."

"Alright, just checking."

John must have disappeared, and yet she still stood in the same spot. Had they really been about to kiss? Surely if they had, Tony would stride back to her and finish what they'd started.

Instead, Tony said, "Do you want to go up first?"

Tony hadn't been able to say no when Jodie suggested going sofa shopping. And now he was paying for it. This whole week, they seemed to keep bumping into each other at work, and when they weren't at The Dog, Jodie was at his house decorating, or meeting with carpenters and builders about his unit and exposing the wall in his bedroom. He'd wanted to spend more time with her, and boy was he. But spending time with her, and not touching her in the way he wanted—not pulling her close and finally kissing her—was becoming impossible.

And now they had spent the past couple of hours driving around different shops, testing out sofas. They were all starting to blend into one, if he were totally honest. But she seemed to be having fun, so that was something. She wanted him to test them all out before he made a decision. Even though he would have been perfectly happy with the first one she had shown him.

Jodie walked them through their fourth shop of the day to find the last two sofa choices. She seemed pretty pleased with herself that she had found two options in one shop. Her hips swayed as she walked, and not for the first time, Tony had to divert his gaze. He had lost control in the cellar. What had got into him, he didn't know. Maybe it was feeling her hand in his, or the way her body had been so close when she had stood back up from under the arch. Maybe it was because being down there had felt like they were hidden from reality, hidden from the world. If he'd been able to inch forward just a bit more, he could have finally tasted her, finally felt how soft her lips were and explored her mouth with his tongue. But John had interrupted. And the look on his face when Tony had stood at the bottom of the cellar steps told him John knew exactly what he had done.

But perhaps that had been a good thing. There wasn't any way that he would have been able to control himself once he had kissed her. No. He needed to avoid that again at all costs. They were, after all, friends. And he certainly couldn't be kissing an employee down in his cellar. He rolled back his shoulders, his muscles tense. Just two more sofas and he could get home, get back to Max and close himself away in the quietness of his house. He needed to be alone.

Jodie stopped at a sofa, one that looked remarkably similar to the other three they had seen so far. "What do you think?" she asked, her hands out wide, presenting it to him for his critique.

Tony searched desperately for something, anything, that made it different to the ones he had seen before.

Jodie groaned and slapped her hands on her thighs, "Please don't say you think it looks like the others?"

Tony nodded slowly. "I'm sorry, this just isn't my thing."

"No, I get it." Although she still looked disappointed. "At least sit on it and see what you think."

He followed her orders. He wiggled a bit, trying to get comfortable.

"And?" She hadn't sat on any of them with him. Every time she'd stood, watching him like a hawk, trying to gauge whether it was 'the one'.

"I mean, it is a bit uncomfortable."

"Really, so this one is off the list? The only one you have actually ruled out so far."

"Yep, think so." He jumped up from the sofa. In truth, it had been fine, but he just wanted to give Jodie something more, something she so obviously wanted from him. And it seemed to do the trick. Even though he had rejected it, she had a big smile on her face and was already looking around for her last sofa pick.

"Over here."

He followed her once more and instantly sat down on the sofa without waiting for her to ask his opinion. It still looked like all the others they had seen. Of course, her keen eye could pick out the subtle differences, but that was why this was her calling in life.

He sat back in the chair, his ankle resting on his knee. That felt nice. Although he had spent the whole afternoon sitting on sofas—or sitting in the car to go to the next shop to sit on a sofa—it was nice to finally sit and feel relaxed. He rested his head back and closed his eyes, ignoring the other shoppers around him. He deserved this little break. He had cleaned out his cellar, he had resisted kissing Jodie and ruining their friendship and had sat on far more sofas then he thought was possible in a day.

A sigh escaped him, and then he felt the seat pad next to him dip.

An arm wrapped around his bicep, and a head rested against his shoulder. He let himself lean into Jodie, enjoying her cuddling into him as if she didn't even need to think about it.

"We found the one," she whispered.

Tony chuckled softly. He sure had.

CHAPTER 18

Jodie was regularly called on at the last minute to cover a shift or help out at busy times at The Dog. She didn't mind getting those last-minute calls and usually accepted. A few days after finding Tony his perfect sofa, Jodie got the call. Ryan had become ill just before the restaurant was about to open for the evening shift, and Jodie accepted without hesitation.

An unseasonal chill was around and dark clouds rolled overhead. Pulling her jacket closer, she walked to The Dog. As always, she peered at Tony's cottage as she passed, noting that his lights were on. Her heart plummeted. Looked like her shift would be spent Tony-less.

A short while into her shift, when she was coming out of the bathroom, Micha called to her. She joined Micha at the hatch where dinners were served.

"Need help taking these out?" Jodie asked, nodding down to the two roast dinners piled high with meat, potatoes and Yorkshire puddings.

"That would be great, thanks. I have a few more coming through. It's for table four." She nodded to the corner. "But I actually wanted to tell you that I've just seated Tony at one of your tables."

"Oh, really?" Jodie turned round and surveyed her little cluster of tables, and spotted him easily. Her eyes were always drawn to his muscular form and those dark eyes. Her heart took a dive bomb when she spotted a petite blonde woman sitting opposite him. Tony was wearing a white dress shirt, pressed to perfection and bulging at his biceps, and smart navy trousers with tan leather shoes. The only thing he was missing was Max.

She forced herself to turn back to Micha with a blank face.

Micha was too busy to even register her expression. "He told me that the woman he's with is from a website; they do lots of advertising and I think they have an award for places like this. I don't know, really. I know it's something business related, but he said it all too quietly. But anyway, the point is, make service the priority. I would have seated them at one of my tables, but I'm overrun."

"Yeah, that's fine," Jodie lied, taking the two dishes and walking behind Micha to serve them at table four. She didn't dare look in Tony's direction. When the dishes had been safely deposited, she took a steadying breath, plastered a fake smile on her face, pulled her notepad and pen from her pocket and made her way to Tony's table, her heart breaking with every step she took.

"Evening," she said to them, forcing a cheery smile and breaking their attention away from their menus. "I'm Jodie and I'll be your waitress tonight."

Tony's eyes had quickly locked onto hers when she spoke, his mouth hanging in shock and his eyes pained. Yep, he had no idea she would be here tonight.

"Can I take your drink order?" she asked them politely.

"A glass of Prosecco for me, please," the woman said.

She was beautiful, Jodie cursed inwardly. Probably what a

lot of men liked in a woman. Small-framed, a tiny hint of curves in her body, and blonde, perfectly coiffed hair with bright red lipstick. Her little black dress hugged her body and her boobs looked ready to pop out.

Jodie noted her drink order and turned towards Tony, who was still gawping.

"The same please," he said quietly.

She could have laughed. Him drinking Prosecco? She noted the 'times two' on her pad.

"Jodie," he added. "I didn't realise you were working tonight."

Did that mean he had arranged this around her usual working schedule? Although Micha said this was for business, it was quite clearly also for pleasure. She almost threw up in her mouth. "I'm just covering for Ryan as he wasn't feeling well." She smiled down at him again, but knew it wouldn't reach her eyes.

"Oh," Tony replied. "Jodie, this is Lexi. Lexi, this is Jodie."

"Hi," Lexi responded sweetly, giving a little wave of her hand.

"Pleasure to meet you," Jodie replied. She had to remind herself that it wasn't Lexi's fault she felt hurt or upset. Lexi was the innocent party, who needed to be impressed. "Have you chosen what you would like to eat, or should I leave you two for a minute?" The words stung her. She didn't want to leave them sitting here intimately in the candlelight.

"I know what I'm having," Lexi said, looking at Tony to see if he was ready too. He nodded at her with a charming smile that had the ability to make Lexi swoon and to kill Jodie at the same time.

"Can I have the Caesar salad please?" Lexi handed her the menu, turning back to Tony.

"Can I have the steak, please? The chef knows how I like it." He handed Jodie the menu, and locked eyes with Lexi. She took it from him, careful not to touch his hand, not wanting to feel the tingles it would send through her body. Their attention had been drawn back to each other, and for now, no one else existed to them.

"Of course." Jodie turned, feeling the croak in her voice, and left them.

Fuck. How was she going to be able to do this? She registered their orders and waited for John to pour the Prosecco.

"You alright?" he asked her.

"Yep," she replied, trying her best to sound like nothing was wrong. John looked past her to Tony and Lexi, seeming to understand. Jodie hated how transparent she obviously was.

All sound seemed to disappear on the way back to the table with their drinks. She set them down carefully, ensuring not a drop was spilt. She picked up the steak knife from her tray that she'd collected for Tony and walked round the back of him, so as to not lean over him and interrupt their conversation. She barely registered that they were talking about the pub and Tony was speaking openly, conversation flowing naturally. Why was he happy to open up to Lexi, yet Jodie had to coax any tiny bit of information out of him? She wanted to take the steak knife and stab it into his splayed hand on the table.

As she leant down to place the knife next to his plate, Tony turned his face to her. "Thank you."

They were close enough that she could just about feel the word on her cheek, smell his familiar aftershave that stung her nose. Tears threatened to surface, and she couldn't even acknowledge him. She finished her task and left them.

She managed to avoid going back over to the table, just monitoring that they had enough to drink. Tony had barely touched his Prosecco, whereas Lexi had consumed most of hers. On the way past to other tables, she tried to ignore

Tony's quick glances while ensuring she seemed professional and approachable if they did need anything else.

Then the shrill ding of the bell summoned her to the serving hatch, where the steak and salad sat waiting for her.

Composed, professional, friendly.

Plastering another smile on her face, she turned around and made her way to their table. Tony eyed her almost immediately, watching her walk towards them, plates in hand. The closer she got to him, the more he tensed. When she reached the table, Lexi looked up with a bright smile and a glint in her eye. She was obviously having a lovely time. Jodie placed the plates in front of them, asking if they would like anything further to drink. Lexi requested another glass of Prosecco, but Tony shook his head.

Just as Jodie was about to retreat to fetch another glass, Lexi asked her a question. "How long have you worked here, Jodie?" She started eating her salad but seemed genuinely interested in the answer.

Tony unfolded his napkin and placed it over his lap, looking between them.

"A few weeks now, I think," Jodie responded.

"Do you like working here?" Lexi shot Tony a look, ensuring he stayed silent during her questioning.

"It's a lovely place," Jodie told her. "And I'm not just saying that because Tony can hear." It was the truth; she couldn't lie even if she wanted to. "Everyone is like family here."

Lexi smiled up at her, but Jodie could tell she was questioning if she was sincere or not.

"Tony and I were just discussing the fact he allows dogs here—what do you think about that?" Lexi's face turned stonier, becoming more calculating by the second.

Jodie weighed up her answer before replying. "I think the fact that the pub and restaurant welcomes everyone, including families and dog owners, gives it a lovely atmosphere." She glanced over at Tony and noticed his jaw clenching, something he usually did when he was agitated or holding back. "Where is Max, by the way?"

Tony opened his mouth to answer, but Lexi butted in first with a fake laugh. "Oh, I don't really like dogs, so Tony kept him at home." Jodie's heart broke even more. If that was even possible.

Lexi's façade was falling before her eyes. Her petite frame and cutesy behaviour had at first masked her manipulative side. But she was about as fake as her boobs seemed to be. Jodie glanced back at Tony, who was still sitting back, staring at Lexi as she spoke, twiddling his almost full glass. Why was he even here, entertaining her?

"I'll go and get you another glass of Prosecco and leave you in peace. Enjoy," she said, and walked away.

What on earth was he playing at? This was so unlike him. Or what she thought she knew about him. She quickly delivered Lexi's drink and rushed away to serve her other tables.

Twenty minutes later, Micha gave her the nod to have a five-minute break while she covered her tables. Jodie needed it. Her back hurt and her feet stung. But not as much as her heart did. She was exhausted, emotionally and physically. She regretted every minute of answering the damn call to pick up this shift.

Closing the door behind her in the stuffy little break room, she leant against the frame, breathing calming breaths in and out. What was she going to do? She desperately didn't want to be here, to witness him with someone else. Her heart shattered every time she saw them. Maybe she could say she was unwell?

No, she knew she wouldn't do that. It wasn't fair to the others who'd have to cover for her.

The door behind her opened, pushing her out of the way.

To her surprise, Tony walked in and closed the door behind him.

"What are you doing?" she asked, backing into the room further.

"I needed to speak with you." He searched her face. "Are you okay?" He took one step towards her and she retreated more, not wanting to be close to him.

"Yeah, I'm fine. Just on my break." She was short and bitey. "I can come and take another drink order in a minute if you like?"

He shook his head. "No. That's not what I want. You seem off?"

"No, I'm fine." She resolutely stood tall, willing herself, just once, not to be an open book for him to read.

He searched her eyes while she stood, still and unmoving, glaring right back at him.

"Can I ask you a favour?" He waited for her to nod. "Can you watch Max for me?"

"What do you mean?" she asked, puzzled.

"Will you have Max overnight for me tonight?" His cheeks coloured a deep red. She had never seen him blush before.

The realisation dawned on her of what he was implying. Forcing herself to remain neutral, she replied, "Of course." She grabbed her house key from her bag and handed it to him. He caught her hand in his when she deposited the key. The normal tingles erupted all over her body, betraying her. But with it also erupted a pain, deep in her stomach. Wrenching her hand from his grasp, she turned away to close her bag. "I'll be late tonight. Let him in and leave the key under the flower pot so I can get in." She rummaged around in her bag, desperately trying to make herself look busy, desperately trying to hide how her world had flipped upside down.

"Thank you." His steps shuffled across the floor and the door opened and closed with a soft click.

What happened to not having women round? What happened to having no room in his life for anyone? Why Lexi? Had that woman really changed it all? Was it because she was blonde and pretty and her tits were on display? Or was it because she could help him raise the profile of this place?

Either way, this was not the Tony she respected and cared for. Or at least, not who she thought he was.

She slumped against the wall, willing tears to not spill. There would be time for that later.

Now, there was only time for working.

When she left the little room, she was glad to see they had gone. Their napkins were thrown on the table, with Tony's almost full glass of Prosecco on top of a twenty pound note. Jodie pocketed the tip and proceeded to clear the table for the next guests. She would put the money in the jar for all the staff to share. She didn't want his pity money.

By the time the last customer had left, and all the tables had been cleared and menus organised, her body ached from head to toe. Her heart throbbed painfully, never letting up. It was past midnight and the night was dark and cloudy, with a cold wind blowing across the green.

She said goodbye to John, who was locking up, and walked to her home. On the way past Tony's cottage, she couldn't help but look to see if the lights were on. She hated the way it hurt her to see his living room light behind the closed curtains. She pulled her jacket around her tighter, dipped her head against the wind and willed her feet to take her home.

As she bent down to get the key from the flower pot, Max whimpered inside. She rushed to open the door to comfort him, and greeted him with open arms. He must be so confused and anxious.

"Hello, boy," she said softly to him. He whimpered again, rubbing his body all over her as she stroked and spoke to him. "It's alright, Max. I'm here." Tony hadn't even switched a light on for him. Max looked just as forlorn and hurt as she felt. She was glad for his presence—at least she could concentrate on him and have some company. As tired as she was, she knew sleep would not come easy tonight.

She closed the living room curtains and poured herself and Max some water. He didn't even want to go out into the garden, instead staying glued by her side, probably fearing she would abandon him too. They went upstairs together and she snuggled him on her bed with fluffy blankets and pillows, hoping that at least one of them would feel better. It was overkill and she was spoiling him, but she wanted to offer him every comfort she could. Maybe if he felt better, she could feel better too.

By the time she got into bed, next to a now-snoring Max, it was past one in the morning. Her bones seemed to ache and creak as she snuggled herself next to him. She had left the curtains open to allow a breeze to sweep over them while they slept. As she looked out across the dark village green, stroking Max, she gazed intently at Tony's now lit bedroom window. She was torturing herself, she knew it, but was unable to prevent herself from doing it.

She watched, transfixed with the sight of the lit window surrounded in darkness. It suddenly flicked off and she felt a tear finally escape and roll down her cheek.

CHAPTER 19

Tony knew he shouldn't have asked Jodie to look after Max.

No.

He shouldn't have agreed to leave Max at home while eating dinner with Lexi. And he should have insisted that they stay at the pub. He should have insisted it wasn't a date. Hell, he should never have contacted Lexi in the first place. That call was a mistake, him trying to convince his stupid, nagging stomach that he needed to do more with the pub, not him longing for more. For a relationship. For Jodie.

He'd fucked up. Again. He continually treated Jodie like shit, giving her mixed messages. They were getting close, he knew that and she must feel it too, and then he showed up with another woman. And then he'd left with that woman. Jodie wouldn't know he hadn't slept with Lexi, Jodie wouldn't know that he'd asked her to leave when he realised his mistake. All she knew was that he'd left with a woman.

Jodie wasn't meant to be there last night—he'd arranged the dinner specifically around her shifts. But who was he kidding? She would have still found out. He paced up and down his living room, ruffling his hair in frustration. He'd hardly slept. He missed Max. He missed Jodie.

Grabbing his keys, he rushed out the door. He needed to tell her. Lay it all on the line.

Heart thundering in his chest, he knocked on Jodie's door. It eventually opened, but she was already retreating back to the sofa when he walked in. She was wearing a pyjama set with little shorts and a strappy top. He was barely able to force his brain into gear, watching her retreating bum wiggle in the shorts.

Max stayed on the sofa. He'd never not greeted Tony before. *Shit*, he had really messed up. With both of them. Jodie pulled a blanket over herself and Max and stared at the telly where *Friends* was playing. Max just looked at him, sorrow in his eyes.

"Morning," he said brightly. Jodie winced at his overly bright demeanour. "You look rough." She'd obviously had trouble sleeping too. He stood by the window, hands in his pockets.

"Thanks," she said, budging Max out of the way so she could cover herself in the blanket properly.

"I didn't mean it like that," he said, trying to backtrack. He didn't mean she wasn't beautiful—she was always beautiful. "I mean you just look tired."

"I always look tired."

"Max," he called out to the dog, who still sat resolutely with Jodie. "You gonna come see me?" He bent down and patted his thighs.

"He's upset with you."

"What do you mean?" he asked, straightening up, pain stabbing at his chest.

Jodie raised her voice, her eyes cold. "You left him here, in the dark, without any food or water. He didn't know what to do with himself. He won't leave my side now, scared that I'm going to abandon him too."

"It was only for one night." He didn't know why he was trying to defend himself. He knew he was in the wrong and he'd come to apologise.

"He doesn't understand that," she shouted back at him. "How do you think that made him feel? Just being ditched for some random woman?" Tears welled in her eyes.

"Max, come here boy." Tony crouched down again, speaking softly. Jodie huffed in annoyance as Max bent his head low and stepped off of the sofa to go to him. Max still loved him, he always would. "I'm sorry, boy." He kissed the dog on top of his head lovingly, hoping that Jodie knew his apology was for her too. "See? All better."

He looked up at her, a smile on his face. But the cold look she gave him told him everything he needed to know. It wasn't going to be that easy to win her over. She turned back to *Friends* without a word. The indifference hurt more than if she'd slapped him in the face.

"I need to speak to you about last night," he said quietly, still stroking Max's ears.

"I don't want to talk about it."

"Please Jodie, it's important."

She scoffed, her gaze not breaking from the TV.

"Jodie, come on. I need to explain—"

She cut him off. "I don't want to hear it."

He needed to make her see, he needed to tell her the truth. So he tried again. "It's about Lexi."

"I don't care. Will you stop going on about it already?" She turned the volume up.

He stood up. He'd come here to set the record straight, but she couldn't even give him the time of day. Frustration at not being heard was starting to bubble up deep inside him. If she could just hear him out for five minutes, just listen to the truth, then he could lay it all out on the table, his feelings and all. He and Jodie were good together, they had fun, they laughed, and despite their occasional bickering, everything was easy with her. He didn't have to put on a front, he didn't have to pretend. She made him rethink everything he'd thought about relationships.

But at this very moment, she wasn't having any of it. He knew this conversation wouldn't be easy, but she was making it way harder than it needed to be.

"Will you just listen?" he snapped. As soon as he said it, he knew he had messed up...*again.*

"Don't you dare speak to me like that!" she thundered at him, finally reaching her breaking point. She jumped up from the sofa. "You have the audacity to abandon Max with me for the night, without any food or even a light on for him, and expect us to welcome you with open arms?"

"Well, Max isn't bothered anymore, is he? And I'm trying to—"

"He's a dog, he doesn't know any better."

Rolling his eyes, he mumbled under his breath, "Next time I won't ask you to look after him, if that's the issue." But Jodie heard it, and she clenched her jaw tight.

"That's not the issue and you know it."

"What's the issue then, Jodie?" If she wanted to speak and not listen to anything he had to say, then she could bloody well talk.

She turned away from him and grabbed a hoodie, putting it on and covering up her heaving breasts. He missed them immediately. Even angry, she was stunning. Even angry, he contemplated pulling her to him and kissing her to make her forget all this.

She shook her head while zipping herself up.

"You're not going to say it, are you?" he said to her back.

"We both know the real issue is that you're jealous. There, I said it for you."

At those words, she swung back around. "Jealous?" She scoffed, trying to brush off his accusation. "That's utter crap."

"No it's not, and you know it. You can't hide anything from me. I can see right through you." The ridiculous thing was, he didn't care if she was jealous—he just wanted her to forgive him. He had just wanted to tell her nothing had happened with Lexi. "The truth is, I—"

"You are so full of yourself."

He rolled his eyes and folded his arms. Why would she just not listen?

His frustration seemed to make her angrier. "It wasn't jealousy you saw last night. It was disgust," she bit at him. "Disgust at how tacky it is to bring a date to your restaurant. Not only that, but to get rid of your dog just because she doesn't like them. I thought you were a better man than that."

"It wasn't a date, it was business."

"It was a date!" she shouted. "How embarrassing in front of all of your staff. You took her home! All of your staff witnessed that. It's disgraceful."

"She's well connected." He tried again. "She can help push The Dog to the next level, she can help develop it as a B&B."

Before he could tell her that he hadn't slept with Lexi, her eyes widened, and her bottom lip trembled. *Fuck.* He hadn't told her about the B&B yet.

"So you took her home to improve business? That's even worse. You're a sellout. I would have more respect for you if you just admitted you wanted a bit of action." She choked on her words, tears spilling out.

He took a steadying breath before responding to her. This was getting out of control and had to stop. "That's enough," he told her in a calmer voice than he felt. "I didn't sleep with Lexi. It wasn't a date."

"And you expect me to believe that." Jodie gave a dark laugh. But it was obvious she didn't think it was the least bit funny. And it was obvious she had no intention of believing him.

He shook his head. Unbelievable. Even with the truth, she didn't want to listen, didn't want to believe him. This was going nowhere. This was proving his point that relationships didn't work. Why did he ever think that would change?

Clenching his jaw, he said, "I suggest you remember that you're my employee and I'm your client, before you say anything else. Otherwise you might find yourself in a predicament you don't want to be in." He let the words sink in for a second. Jodie didn't move, didn't speak. "Max, come!" he bellowed and walked out the door, Max following obediently behind.

The pain in his chest felt like he had just cut out his heart and left it on Jodie's living room floor.

CHAPTER 20

Jodie ran around the house, shoving away last-minute clutter. She didn't really have to worry how her house looked around Mark—he wouldn't care one bit if it was a pigsty—but she cared. And he was about to turn up any second, so she quickly plumped her cushions and took her cup of tea out to the sink.

Yesterday, when she was torn in two over what had happened with Tony, she had called on her oldest friend and sobbed her heart out. Kelsie had been supportive as always, just listening and letting Jodie get it all out. And then she had been practical. "Jodie, I know you're hurting, but this pain will pass. You know that, don't you?" Jodie just mumbled. "These things always work out. And it has to, seeing as you work for him."

"What on earth am I going to do when I next see him at work?" Jodie bashed her head against the fluffy cushion on her sofa. She hadn't left it since Tony marched out of her home with Max.

"You are going to be calm and professional. You will hurt inside, there isn't any way to get around that. But you don't have to show him that. Don't give him the satisfaction that he's right, and that you are jealous."

"I'm not jealous!" Jodie protested, biting her thumb.

"Jodie…seriously? It's me you're talking to. I'm not saying it's a bad thing that you're jealous. It just happens when you're friends with a guy. Our hearts aren't as clever as our heads, Jodie. But at least you know where you stand now…and that means you can move on, that you can heal."

She sighed. "I'm not sure this pain will ever go."

"It will do. I promise that. But it just takes time. And unfortunately with working for him and having to see him, it will take longer for you to get over your crush. But just think of it this way—you didn't move there to find love. You moved there to live your dream life, to set up your business. You don't need a distraction. And men are definitely a distraction! Tony was never part of your plan Jodie, and I'm sorry to say it sounds like he never will be."

Jodie shed a silent tear. Kelsie was right. But that didn't mean it was any less painful. That the knife that had been lodged in her heart since last night didn't keep twisting and turning and hurting her more.

"Listen," Kelsie continued, "how about I get Mark to pop down tomorrow to have a look at your shower situation? He was going to finish early anyway, so he can be with you in the afternoon. If he has a look now and gets everything measured up and ordered, he can fit it in an evening or a weekend. How about that?"

"Oh, you don't have to do that, Kelsie. It's fine really."

"No it's not. I can't give you a hug right now, and God knows when I'll actually be able to come and see you. This is the only thing I can do to make you feel better. So it's happening. No arguments." Kelsie had put her foot down. She was just as stubborn as Tony was. That knife twisted around again.

"Okay, well in that case it sounds great." At least it was something to look forward to.

Now Jodie had just finished washing her cup when a heavy knock sounded at her door.

She opened the door to find Mark on the pavement, staring out over the green. She joined him, wiping her wet hands on a tea towel. God, it was nice to have someone here that she knew. Instantly her heart felt lighter. She greeted him with a hug and he squeezed her back.

"Kelsie sends a hug too," he told her. "She's gutted she can't be here."

"She's going to badger you for all the details." Jodie laughed, knowing what Kelsie would be like when Mark returned.

He nodded in agreement. "Beautiful place you've stumbled across." He folded his arms, the tattooed snakes and demons covering them twitching over his bulging muscles, and looked back out at the green.

"Isn't it?" She turned around to admire Winton Green as well. "And so peaceful." They stood for a moment listening to the birds chirping and the breeze through the trees.

"How are you feeling now? Kels filled me in."

Jodie smiled. She had known Mark for years now, ever since he and Kelsie had first met. But they didn't talk about things like this, about feelings. He was obviously trying his best to be a dutiful friend in place of Kelsie.

"I'll be alright." She shrugged. "Being here has changed me."

"In what way?"

"I care." She ran her fingers over her lips. "I never cared in London. I never wanted someone before. Sure, I always thought it would be nice to have someone one day and have a family, but I never pursued anyone and I never got hurt."

"Do you really think the countryside has changed that, or do you think it was this Tony?"

134

Jodie was shocked. Kelsie would be proud of him. She contemplated her answer for a moment. "I don't know," she admitted. "Anyway, you're here to give me a bathroom, not life advice." She smiled up at him, changing the conversation to a more light-hearted one.

"Alright then. What do you want?"

"I need a bloody shower!" she told him.

"I thought it smelled a bit funny round here." He laughed at his own joke.

"Ha ha," she replied dryly. "They only had a bath installed and I thought I could live with it a while longer, but I can't. It's a—" She stopped. Mark had averted his eyes above her head and she could feel a presence behind her. Her heart shrank.

She turned around and Max found her waiting hand, sniffing and wiggling at her, wanting all of her attention. But it was Tony who had that. He took large, confident strides towards them, and even from this distance she could see his jaw was clenched. He held Mark's gaze above her head and Jodie felt the atmosphere harden around her. Maybe by some miracle she would shrink into a tiny speck of dust and completely avoid this situation.

"Hi," she said to Tony as he reached them, breaking his attention away from Mark. He snapped his head towards her, a look on his face she couldn't decipher.

"Hi," he replied softly, but his muscles were tense beneath his navy blue polo shirt, and his hands fisted. "Can I speak to you for a moment?"

"I'm a bit busy," she replied, indicating Mark.

Tony glanced at Mark, who hadn't yet broken his stare, and made the slightest of eye movements down to Mark's ring finger, checking for a wedding band.

Jodie smiled to herself. Mark didn't wear his wedding band on his finger in case it got damaged when he was working— instead he opted to wear it hidden on a chain under his shirt.

He also wasn't wearing any branded clothing or driving his work van.

There was no way for Tony to know if he was working for Jodie, or if their relationship was something else. Tony clenched his jaw some more. It shouldn't have made her happy, but it did.

Touché.

Tony looked back at her, his dark eyes sad. "It won't take long."

"I'm busy now. We can talk another time." She turned around to Mark. "Shall we go in?"

"I'd love to," he replied, smiling down at her. Mark knew exactly who was standing in front of him, and he seemed to be enjoying the torment they were unleashing on him just as much as she was. He put one hand on Jodie's back, nothing inappropriate, but enough to annoy Tony further.

They left Tony on the pavement, staring after them. Max whimpered beside him. Sure, it was sadistic, but she relished putting Tony in a predicament he didn't want to find himself in.

Mark spent an hour at Jodie's, planning out the bathroom. He was pretty confident he'd be able to get a shower unit installed within a week. It wouldn't look pretty but it would at least function. And then a few weeks after that, he just might be able to sort the rest of it out. Jodie was ecstatic, relieved at the prospect of having a shower. It would change everything.

As she was going back inside after saying goodbye to Mark, her phone started to vibrate in her pocket.

Looking down at the caller ID, her old work number flashed up on screen. What could they be calling for?

"Hello."

"Hello, babe!" Ashley's shrill voice erupted from the phone. She and Jodie had been good friends back in London, but had hardly spoken since Jodie left. She was PA to the director. "How are you doing? Are you bored there yet?"

"I'm alright. How's it going in London?"

"Great! I met someone. His name is Andrew. He's such a hunk; I adore him."

Jodie wanted to bang her head against the wall. Ashley had always been a bit self-centered. Trust her to pick this time to gloat that she had someone. She carried on listing out reasons why Andrew was a spectacular boyfriend, and Jodie glazed over.

"Anyway," Ashley had hardly taken a breath of air, "I was ringing about work…"

"Okay," Jodie muttered, unsure of where this was going.

"They wanted me to call you to see if you'll come in for a meeting. They miss you and regret letting you go."

"What?" She was stunned.

"They want to hire someone in a more managerial position and your name is at the top of the list."

"B-but what about the redundancies?" she stuttered, her head spinning.

"Apparently it will be a completely new role, so the redundancies don't matter. Anyway, can you come in tomorrow?"

"Tomorrow?" This was all happening so quickly. Her mind went into overdrive.

"Just say you'll come in?" Ashley pleaded. "Just hear them out. I miss you."

Jodie tried to process her thoughts. She had never thought about returning to London before. Now doubt crept in. Maybe this life wasn't for her…maybe this was her lifeline to get back to normal and stop pretending. She swallowed. "Okay," she said.

Ashley's shriek pierced her eardrum. "Oh, I can't wait to see you!" she shouted. "Can you get up here for twelve? They want to take you out for lunch."

Jodie nodded, and then realising Ashley couldn't see she confirmed the plans.

They hung up shortly afterwards and Jodie slumped back on the sofa, dazed. Then she shouted, "Shit!" and jumped up, running upstairs. She needed an outfit.

~

Tony let the water run over his body, trying to wash away that bubbling rage. He'd been angry ever since his argument with Jodie. It had got so out of hand and he kept replaying his words in his head. How had it gone from him wanting to tell her how he felt—really felt—to him telling her they were only friends and, more importantly, that he was now her boss?

He turned the heat up even more, scalding his skin to try and feel something else. His selfishness, his behaviour, his guilt was eating him up. And to top it all off, Jodie wouldn't even speak to him.

She'd had him in a spin ever since he saw her that first day, when he didn't even know her name. He wanted her. Badly. But more than that, he needed her as his friend. She had made him open up more than anyone had before. She had wiggled herself into his life, and now that she was gone, there was a gaping hole.

He turned the shower off and dried himself. Yesterday, when he saw her with that man, his heart had exploded, his body searing with jealousy, wanting to claim her as his. But she wasn't. And she couldn't be.

They had to just be friends. He couldn't condemn her to a life with him, living like his parents did. All the love gone, just going through the motions of life with no passion or friendship. But he couldn't live without her either, so no matter if it hurt him every time he looked at her, no matter if he had to hide his feelings. Having her as his friend was better than not having her at all.

He got dressed and walked over to her house, Max trotting beside him, tail wagging happily. The closer they got, the harder his heart beat. This time, he had to talk to her.

She walked out of her gate just as he reached her cottage.

"Wow." He couldn't hold it in.

She wore a navy wrap dress that clung to every inch of her body, hugging her breasts, causing a deep, plunging v, shaping the curve of her hips and waist. Her bright red heels stopped on the pavement as he stood gawping at her. Stunning.

"You look….amazing," he breathed, taking a step forward, wanting to be closer to her.

"Thanks." She blushed, stroking Max hello.

"Where are you heading dressed like that?" He was still staring her up and down, hungrily. That rage that had been bubbling in him turned to jealousy.

"London."

His eyes snapped up to hers in alarm. "London? Are you meeting that man again?"

"No, Mark is my friend and was looking at my bathroom." She brushed something off of her dress. "My old company wants a meeting with me," she explained.

"What do you mean?" He couldn't stop the desperate note from also escaping.

She shrugged. "They called and asked me to meet with them. They want to discuss me going back to a more senior role."

"Going back?" He was still in a state of shock.

"Yeah."

"But you can't."

"What do you mean, I can't?" she asked him, haughtily.

"You haven't given this place a chance yet," he tried to reason with her. She couldn't leave him.

"I have to keep my options open," she replied quietly, shrugging. "It's my future I'm trying to figure out."

"But..." he began.

"I have to go, Tony," she said softly, avoiding his eyes. "I'll be late otherwise." She walked to her car, leaving him and Max staring after her, Tony's heart in the pit of his stomach.

CHAPTER 21

Jodie emerged from her lunch meeting three hours after it had started, utterly...drained. It had been nice to see her old boss Darren again, and getting to know the new boss David more.

They had talked back and forth about the role they envisaged Jodie stepping into, complimenting her on why they thought she was perfect for the role—her work ethic, her professional behaviour, her ingenious ideas. She'd had no idea they valued her so much when she worked there.

She was open with them throughout, letting them know why she had left, her dreams of owning her own business, of making it successful. It probably looked like she was playing hardball when she discussed with them the fact she would have to sell her cottage and move back to London, and how she might not be able to afford a place there. And then they had increased their offer a few times during the course of the meeting, trying to entice her. It hadn't been her intention to barter with them. She was just trying to gain some clarity in her head, to be able to decide either way.

Driving home, she mulled everything over, her thoughts travelling faster than the car. Pulling up in front of her cottage, she turned the ignition off, taking a minute to absorb the silence and peace around her. She needed it after being in London. Being there was like a poison invading her body.

Leaning against the headrest, she closed her eyes, letting her shoulders drop the couple of inches they had hiked up. She was stressed. The warm sunshine spilled onto her skin, relaxing her for just a moment.

Breathing the last of her held breath out, she opened the car door, hardly surprised when Tony appeared along the road with Max. He seemed twitchy and agitated, whereas she was calm.

"Let me guess," she called to him. "You want to talk?"

He nodded, his jaw clenching under his stubble. Jodie let them all into the house, and before she could even shut the door he started talking.

"You can't move back to London," he began. "You haven't given this place and your business nearly enough time to succeed. It took me months to feel comfortable when setting up the pub, and I still worry at any moment it could all be ruined. You can do this if you try; you just have to give it time. At least you have the waitressing job to bring a bit of money in, and I just know you're on the brink of getting another design contract. Going back to London is a cop-out and you deserve to give your dream a go." He rambled on, hardly breathing, pacing back and forth, not even looking at her to see if she was listening. "You told me you hated living in London and always wanted to escape. To think you would even consider going back is so against who I thought you were. You told me I was wrong for having a date at my business, but going back to London is just as bad. You can't, Jodie! You just can't." All coherent words seemed to fail him.

He stopped his pacing and looked at her, pain evident in his dark eyes. She looked at him calmly, a slight smirk on her face at his outpouring of emotion. He cared about her.

"Finished?" she asked him.

"I just—" He tried to begin again but was silenced when she bent down to remove her heels. He watched her, mesmerised, his coffee eyes turning all black, as she eased the unforgiving shoes from her. She let out a little hiss as she placed the aching balls of her feet on the floor. She hadn't thought taking her shoes off would be an erotic act, but the silent, brooding form of Tony suggested otherwise. He couldn't seem to tear his eyes from her, staring at her hungrily.

"I'm not going back to London," she told him.

He shook his head. "What?" Confusion flashed across his face.

"I'm staying here," she confirmed.

"But you had a meeting in London?"

"Yes. And I decided not to take what they offered. I haven't given this place enough time and I don't want fear to run my life for me and send me back to London, to a place and job I didn't like, just to avoid failure."

"You're really staying?" he asked her, frowning.

"Yep." She laughed gently at his confusion. "I told them at the end of the meeting. How silly do you feel?"

He shot her a look. "Very." He slumped back on the sofa, his large frame sagging as if he were a deflated balloon. Jodie sat next to him, her body turned towards him.

"It was tempting," she admitted. "But going back just reiterated how much I disliked being there." She took a chance —kicking fear to the curb once more—and held his hand that he had placed on his thigh. "I just had to keep my options open."

"God," he muttered. "I was really..." He cut off, apparently unable to find the words.

"Shall I get you some water?" she asked, getting up from the sofa.

He didn't let go of her fingers. He pulled her gently back using her hand and in one smooth motion picked her up and placed her straddled over his lap, the tension palpable in his eyes. She was taken aback by the sudden change of position and his strength. He cradled her face with one slightly rough hand, running his thumb across her jaw and up to her lips. His other hand held her hip in place with firm command.

"Jodie," he whispered. "I was scared you were leaving." He brushed his thumb back and forth over her lip. She couldn't break away from his gaze. "I swear nothing happened with Lexi."

The stark reminder of a few nights ago was too much for Jodie, taking her completely out of her trance and into reality. It felt uncomfortable and stupid straddling his lap. She made a move to vacate her seat, but his hand gripped her firmly in place and his other hand directed her to face him again. "I swear we only talked, and we only talked business."

Jodie gulped down the lump in her throat. So he had been telling the truth. Even though she was relieved to hear it, her heart still broke. All she'd ever wanted him to do was talk to her, open up. Hearing he had spent hours just talking to Lexi still felt like a betrayal that she wasn't sure she could bear. "That's more than you've ever done with me."

"It's not, Jodie," he pleaded. "I'm an open book to you." He tried to meet her shifting gaze. She scoffed. "I am," he persisted. "I've never been so open as I have been with you. I know you may feel differently, but I don't let people in. But you...you're different."

She met his gaze and her heart longed for him. Longed to hear and trust the words he was saying. Longed for any sort of connection with him. Now her fear held her back.

He carried on. "I've never wanted to spend time with anyone before. I've never just made up excuses to see someone. For Christ's sake, I'm paying you to decorate my house just so I can see you. And sure, having a nicely decorated house will be great, and what you're doing has already exceeded my expectations. But I wouldn't have anyone else do it, Jodie. It's because it's you."

Her wall of fear began to crumble, the shields she had put up around her heart lowering.

"I've spent the whole afternoon worrying you might turn your back. About that man I saw you with. And yes, I know you said he's a friend and is doing work for you. But I just can't shake this." He flapped his hands in front of his chest and wrinkled his face up. It was the cutest face she'd ever seen him pull, like he truly didn't know what he was feeling. And for once she could read him, could tell exactly what he felt... because it was what she felt too.

In that moment she took charge. Cupping his cheeks with her hands, she pushed her mouth abruptly against his. After a moment of surprise he sighed and melted into their kiss, wrapping his arms around her.

"Jodie," he whispered when they broke apart. "I don't date. I'm sorry." He rested his forehead against hers. "I've always been a bachelor, there isn't space in my life for a girlfriend or a wife or a family. I don't want to lead you on. I've tried to resist you. Tried to protect you. You deserve so much more."

It wasn't news to Jodie, yet it still stung. She had fallen for someone who was emotionally unavailable and yet she couldn't untangle him from her life. And she didn't want to.

In answer, she sank down further onto his lap. She had been sitting up on her haunches, trying to avoid becoming too intimate with him. Now as she sank fully onto him, his eyes lit with passion and his breath hitched as he felt her. Her gaze held his, trying to convey how she felt where she knew words would fail her.

"I can't promise you anything, Jodie. I can't promise you a future, a ring or even next week."

She knew she may come to regret this decision in the days to come. "Then don't," she replied. "One night is better than none." She kissed him again, wanting to quiet the side of her brain that warned her against this.

"I'll give you everything tonight," he breathed.

She knew he meant it. "Promise?"

"I promise." With her still straddled across him, he sprung up from the sofa. Cupping her bum to keep her close, he ascended the stairs holding her in place. She wrapped herself tighter against him.

"This is dangerous," she giggled in his ear, enjoying the sight of goosebumps that appeared down his neck.

"I've got you," he whispered back. "Trust me."

She forced all doubt and logic from her brain and relished in the moment. She trusted him.

Max stayed sitting at the bottom of the stairs. He had the good sense to stay put.

When they went into her bedroom, Tony knocked the door closed with the heel of his foot and walked over to the bed, throwing her down in front of him and drinking in the sight of her, his eyes dark as night. Then he jumped on the bed himself, kneeling between her legs and bending down to kiss her neck and nibble her ear. She wrapped her arms around his large frame, willing him on.

Then her eyes suddenly sprang open and she tried to wriggle from underneath him.

"What?" he asked, momentarily stopping his caresses.

"I just need to do something," she said, still moving under his body, embarrassment heating up her cheeks.

"What?" he asked again, a devilish glint in his dark eyes.

"I need to get changed," she told him, trying to free herself.

He chuckled and tried to go back to kissing her neck. "That's the opposite of what you need to be doing."

"Tony," she said, dodging his affections. "I need to get changed."

"Why?" He sucked her earlobe.

"I'm wearing Spanx," she admitted. "I need to take them off."

"No you don't," he told her, still not moving his body from her.

"They aren't sexy!" Of all the times she had imagined this scenario, not ever considering it would come true, not one of them had her wearing Spanx.

"I'll be the judge of that," he growled. Pinning her arms either side of her head, he trailed kisses down her body. "Now please tell me I can unwrap you?"

All she could do was nod her head. Her favourite dress was a real wrap dress. It hugged every inch of her body and made her feel sexy as hell.

Kneeling up, he proceeded to untie the strings on the side of her dress, then peeled back the first layer to reveal one of her breasts in a lacy grey bra. He slowly removed the second layer to reveal her body underneath.

He ogled her. "You're telling me *this* isn't sexy?"

She blushed under his hungry gaze. To her embarrassment, her nude-coloured Spanx were on full show, fitting snugly underneath her bra and sucking her body in.

"You're telling me *this* isn't sexy?" he repeated. He bent down and rubbed a finger against one of her nipples through her bra. It wasn't a practical choice, but always made her feel powerful and exotic when she wore it. Her nipple hardened under his touch.

His eyes travelled south and she saw him draw his breath in sharply when he observed the Spanx material rising high on her hips. "Is this a thong?" he asked in bewilderment and flipped her over before she could answer. He threw back her dress to expose the thong riding between her cheeks.

"You're telling me *this* isn't sexy?" he breathed over her bum, kissing and biting her pert bottom. She shivered into her bedspread in response.

With one finger, he traced the material from between her cheeks up and over her hip, then flipped her back over so his finger could travel down the other side toward her private parts. Then his eyebrows rose in astonishment. She drew in her breath, knowing what he had spotted.

"You're telling me *this* isn't sexy?" He ripped open the two poppers between her legs.

Had Spanx ever been so sexy? Pushing the material higher up her body, he completely revealed her private parts while the rest of her body stayed covered. She breathed heavily, anticipating his next move.

Trailing kisses up her thigh, he parted her with his fingers, then kissed her folds while plunging his fingers deep into her, making her clasp the bedspread. She had longed for this moment and never dared believe it would ever happen. He used his tongue to circle her and pulsed his fingers, enticing her further.

Unable to control herself, she gripped his hair to keep him in place, not believing herself capable of such a dominant act. He groaned and then stepped up his pace, bringing her to an earth-shattering climax.

She eased her fingers in his long hair and let her breath catch up while he crawled up her body, staring at her possessively.

"Are you on contraception?" His voice was husky.

"The implant," she breathed heavily, managing to point to her upper inner arm. He tugged the dress off of her shoulder to reveal the spot where it was just visible.

He kissed the little area before asking, "Are you clean?" She nodded again, fixated on him. "I am too," he replied, and she understood what he was implying. She wanted all of him, nothing to get between them. She nodded, knowing he wouldn't want that either.

Rising up once more, he ripped his shirt off, revealing the beautiful body beneath. His muscles rippled and he had a trail of hair leading her down…

"Tony!" she gasped suddenly, jumping from the bed. "The curtains." The curtains were wide open and she didn't trust that if anyone were to walk past they would be hidden. Running round to the window she tried to cover her modesty as best she could. Just as she managed to close the curtains overlooking them, Tony yanked her back onto the bed, with strength that took her breath away.

She lay again, under his ravaging gaze, pinned to the bed and unable to move a muscle, as if he had tied her to the bed itself. He unhooked his belt and pulled it from his jean loops, then undid the button and lowered the zipper. Next he hooked his thumbs into the top of his jeans and tugged them down, revealing the extent of him. Her eyes grew.

Taking off his shoes and socks, he was now fully naked, while she was still covered apart from her privates. He was a god. His muscles rippled in his toned stomach, his tanned skin smooth.

Pulling herself into a seated position, she lowered her mouth onto him. Wanting and needing to taste him, like he had her. She looked up at him through her lashes, and his eyes widened in wonder, twinkling down at her. He looked at her like she was a goddess, a prized possession. Taking him in for a few strides, she savoured him, memorising every part of him.

Pulling the dress off her arms, he threw it to the side and allowed her to pleasure him for a little while longer before lifting her head and lowering her down onto her back.

He rolled the Spanx up a little further and instead of moving to her, he yanked her down, positioning himself right at her entrance. Kneeling back, he hooked one of her legs over his arm and twisted the other around his side.

Then he entered her slowly, allowing them both to absorb the feeling completely. Relishing their act of finally being together, he smiled down at her. Lovingly. Sinfully. He pushed himself in, all the way in, and then all the way out. Her body simmered all over and moans and groans escaped her that she had no control over. He quickened his pace, thrusting quickly, beginning to lose control of himself too. Her moans grew louder, her thrusts matching his, spurring him on.

Grunting, he hooked her leg over his shoulder and tumbled on top of her, still thrusting in and out. They kissed passionately, Jodie biting on his lip to try to contain some of her noises. They took each other up and up, until they came together in a blinding orgasm.

Their pace slowed, but didn't stop completely. Their breath mingled, their bodies slick with sweat.

"That was amazing," she breathed, still clutching him to her.

"Yeah," he whispered, unable to make coherent sentences.

He eventually rolled away, leaving her cold in his wake. Pulling her over to him, he nestled her head in the crook of his neck, the place she had loved so much when they'd shared that nap together.

His hand circled her back, still clad in her underwear. "You're exquisite," he told her, whispering the words into her hair. Resting her hand on his chest, she smiled to herself as she snuggled into him.

Drowsiness swept over them, each keeping the other warm.

CHAPTER 22

Jodie was snuggled up tight against him, still clad in her bra with her Spanx rolled up. The exposed skin of her thighs burned into his, imprinting on him. How could he be so fulfilled yet need more at the same time?

He hadn't meant to sleep with her. Ever. He had just wanted to tell her to stay here, in his life forever, just friends. But when she had sunk herself onto him, fire burning in her eyes, he couldn't resist her anymore and he had taken everything she gave.

She stirred. "Is Max alright?" she whispered.

"He should be." He loved that she always thought of Max.

"I'm going to go and see how he is," she told him, slipping out from underneath the blanket he'd covered them in as she slept.

He turned to lie on his stomach and somehow managed to keep his eyes closed. If he saw her again, there was no doubt she wouldn't be leaving the room.

Sighing contentedly, he couldn't help but think about her, her body squirming beneath him, her eyes searing into his as she tasted him. He hardened under the blanket. *Shit*, he needed her again.

He slipped into another sleep, filled with dreams of Jodie's body sliding underneath his, but soon stirred at her shuffling in the bedroom. She lifted the blanket, wrapping them back up in it, and traced his back muscles with her fingernails, making him shiver at her touch.

"I got you some water."

"Thanks," he croaked, sitting up to take the glass from her. She continued stroking his pecs and abs. "When did you put this on?" he asked, tugging at the white dressing gown with small pink flowers covering her beautiful body. He put the glass on her bedside table.

"When I went to check on Max." She nibbled at his ear lobe.

Little electric sparks shot around his body, straight to his groin. He groaned in pleasure as she started kissing and sucking at his neck. She pushed him onto his back, straddling him and continuing on her path, and he growled his approval.

"When did you take your underwear off?" he asked, peeking at her gaping robe and seeing that her underwear was now gone.

"Before I came in here," she replied, not stopping her kisses and tickles.

"I haven't seen you naked yet."

She sat up on him, a wicked smile on her face. Untying the knot on her robe, she pulled the fabric away from her body. He watched as she revealed herself to him, confident and beautiful, her skin glowing. Pure perfection. Taking the robe off completely, she threw it to the floor.

Now she straddled him, fully naked and in control. He grinned up at her, enjoying this sexy confidence he had never witnessed in her before. She leant over him, grazing his erection, and pushed her perfectly pert boobs onto his hard body. Fuck, she was hot. Taking his wrists in her hands, she pinned them either side of his head, solely in control for once. His body burned with a fierce need. How easy it would be to flip her over and dominate her. But he had the feeling letting her be in control meant a lot more.

Shimmying her hips, she adjusted her position so that she could slide down on him without using her hands. He groaned, feeling her stretching to accommodate him. She whimpered with need and he fought back the urge to take control and push all the way in.

Their eyes never broke from each other's as she rocked back and forth on him hungrily, reading him, what he liked and what he wanted. He just wanted her. And forever wouldn't be long enough.

At first she moved painfully slowly, teasing them both at the same time, but she gradually grew quicker and quicker as the sensations became too much to not give into.

Their breaths came in pants, Tony's thrusts matching hers. She reared up on his body, allowing him to see her completely. She had released his wrists and he grabbed her bum cheeks to help guide her and slam her down onto him.

He sensed that she was close to coming, her head thrown so far back that her brown waves tickled his thighs. He helped her over the edge, and she screamed out in ecstasy, her nipples hardening even more. He continued holding on and pumping inside her, making her feel every moment of her climax, before finally coming himself.

She slumped onto him, exhausted and hot, her breathing as ragged as his own. After a minute, she rolled off him and onto her back. He snuggled into her neck and pulled her into him, not wanting a moment away from that glorious body.

After a while, he said, "We should eat."

She mumbled sleepily in agreement.

"I'll pick up some burgers from the pub, and grab my things from home." He couldn't leave her. Not yet.

"You're going to stay here tonight?" she asked, surprised.

"I promised you the night." He kissed her neck. "If that's okay with you?" He propped himself on his elbow to stare down at her, twisting her wavy hair around one of his fingers.

"Of course."

He noticed the look of hope glimmering in her beautiful green eyes. He was an arsehole.

Getting up from the bed, he pulled his clothes on. That look of hope killed him—he knew it wouldn't last long before it was replaced with pain and disgust. "I'll call John to put the order through. And I'll leave Max with you."

Jodie watched him intently.

"You sure you're okay?" he asked. He had to give her the choice to stop this now before they were in too deep. Maybe she'd have the good sense to say no. But she just nodded. "Okay. I won't be long." He leant down and kissed her cheek. *Fuck*, this was going to be hard.

CHAPTER 23

Tony closed the bedroom door and Jodie let out the sigh she had been holding in. She would not think about all the reasons this was a terrible idea. She had made her bed and she was going to lie in it...with Tony. A beaming smile spread across her face.

She took a bath while he was gone to get clean and ready for his return. Her body still tingled from his touch. She was going to take everything he offered her, savour it all, and remember it when he left. But for now, she would enjoy every second of being his, knowing she would never feel it again.

When he returned, she had already prepared the plates for the much-anticipated food. She was ravenous.

They hardly spoke during dinner, both happy to focus on eating and refuelling. It seemed that they had crossed into a new territory where that awkward chemistry had disappeared, replaced with a comfortable silence.

As she washed their plates, he wrapped both his arms around her from behind. "Do you want to watch something on telly?" he asked into her ear.

She nodded, not really caring but wanting to spend as much time with him as possible.

"What do you want to watch?" They started to sway back and forth, as if dancing to some unheard music.

"I really don't mind; whatever you fancy."

"I'll see what's on." He retreated to the living room.

They ended up watching a nature documentary. She snuggled into Tony's body, David Attenborough's dulcet tones and slow-moving shots soon sending her in and out of sleep. She would drift off and start thinking about Tony and the forbidden thoughts she had told herself not to think about. Then she would jolt awake at the sound of crashing waves or the roar of a predator.

In the moments of almost dreaming, she thought how silly she was to put herself in this position. She was stupid if she thought she'd be able to protect her heart. Sleeping with him would complicate things tenfold, and probably end all chances of them ever being friends. Yet in the next moment, she thought about the possibility that he might want her again one day. She could wear the navy wrap dress and her high heels if she ever wanted to entice him again. Surely he would never be able to look at her again in that dress without having some sort of reaction?

What a sad state of existence that would be. Living from one hookup to the next, with him never wanting her fully. Could she really live like that and be happy?

"Jodie?" he whispered, stroking her arm. "You're sleeping. Let me get you to bed." He made a move to get off of the sofa.

"No," she moaned. "I'm awake." She couldn't even open her eyes as she said it.

Laughing, he dragged her up by the hand and guided her sleepily up the stairs. Depositing her in the bathroom, he promised to bring water back up while she brushed her teeth. When they crossed paths in the hallway so Tony could use the bathroom, he leant down and kissed her lightly on the cheek. Such a simple gesture that sent sparks flying across her body.

By the time they met back in bed, she wasn't on the verge of falling asleep. He pulled her closer to him, kissing and stroking her, and she shivered under his touch. As he kissed her, his tongue swirling with hers, she groaned. He had lit her inner fire once more.

Breaking off their kiss, he rested his forehead against hers. "You'll be sore in the morning," he told her, trying to stop their passion building.

It was already too late. "It's worth it." She kissed him before he could refuse any more. As she drew back from him, she nibbled at his lower lip, bringing it back with her teeth. His eyes were ablaze.

"Tony?" she whispered.

"Yes?" His eyes bored into hers.

"Can I ask you to do something?" A heat rose from her core, up through her chest and into her cheeks. Why did she always have to blush?

"Anything." When she hesitated to reply, he stroked her chin and cheek with his thumb. "Do you know when you blush, it doesn't just show on your cheeks?" She shook her head, captivated by his hungry eyes. "It shows all over your body. Especially on your breasts." He stroked the places her blush was present. "I won't ever be able to look at you blushing again without thinking about that."

"Tony?" she breathed again. He continued looking at her, waiting for her to overcome her shyness, giving her all the time in the world to build her courage. "Can you make love to me?" she whispered.

She saw her words register with him, and was unsure of what his expression meant. Did he pity her, or did he not want to? This was her only chance. He had promised her everything, for this one night only. If she didn't ask now for this one thing, just for him to pretend he loved her and show her in the most intimate way, she would always regret it. It would be an experience that she'd never forget, and in her loneliest, darkest moments, would be able to remember.

Waiting for him to speak, her embarrassment swallowed her up, her hopes dying every second he delayed responding.

He never spoke a word, only brought one hand up behind her head to bring her mouth to his in a tender, soft kiss. Gradually he swept his tongue across her lips, enticing her to open her mouth to him, their tongues wrapping together.

He traced lines and circles down her body from her neck, then cupped her breasts with firm pressure, massaging them and rubbing her nipples. As his hand descended to her hip, he pushed her further back on the bed, pressing his weight on top of her and sliding his legs between hers. Using his thighs to ease her legs apart, he positioned himself at her entrance. Bending his head lower to kiss a trail down to her breasts, he took time loving each one of her nipples.

Sparks shot across Jodie's eyes at his caresses and tingles spread across her body, fire simmering deep within. He kissed her, harder than before, passion bubbling in him too. Pushing at her slowly, entering her inch by inch, he allowed her tender flesh to get used to another intrusion.

Unable to control her desire, she thrust up, wanting more of him, but every time she did, he withdrew a little further, denying her attempt to take control and get lost in their thrusts. "Steady," he growled, holding her hips still while returning to kiss her.

He was giving her what she had asked for...love. And yet her senses were so heightened she was desperate to move and respond.

When he was in all the way, he moved his hands back up to her head, twisting his fingers in her hair as they met their slow thrusts in sync. Their breath tangled, their hearts beating as one. Wrapping her legs around his large frame, she lost herself with him, knowing nothing more than his body, his breathing, his heartbeat.

Their pace quickened as the sensations grew, yet they continued embracing and kissing, working as one. Her body screamed to be released, to shatter around him, yet she resisted, desperate for this moment to take all night, just so their last time never had to end.

He whispered ever-so-gently in her ear, "Come with me." And with his prompt, they tumbled over the edge together, shattering at the seams.

He stayed where he was for a long time, their heartbeats slowing together, their ragged breath becoming normal. He eventually slipped away from her, but curled her up against him.

They didn't say a word. Nothing would be appropriate. They both knew this was the last time.

A single tear rolled down Jodie's cheek.

CHAPTER 24

Jodie gradually awoke from sleep the next morning, stretching out in her bed, having enjoyed the best sleep she'd had since moving to Winton Green. Coming to, she thought about Tony, already instinctively knowing he wasn't in her bed. But she couldn't resist looking, just in case. Her heart still sank as she saw the empty space—he must have bolted the first chance he got.

Rolling over onto his side of the bed, she lay on his cold pillow, his scent wafting around her. Yesterday was the best experience she'd ever had with a man, by far. She had given herself fully to him and there was no doubt in her mind he had given everything to her too. Just like he'd promised. She had no regrets about that. One amazing night with him would be better than never experiencing that.

Yet her heart wasn't as smart as her head. Would she be able to stay friends with him without falling madly and deeply in love? If not, working with him and being his friend was about to turn extremely awkward.

The next time she saw him was bound to be embarrassing. And maybe they needed to talk about keeping it quiet too, so it didn't become gossip around the pub and locals. What would everyone say about that juicy story?

The bedroom door opened with a thud and Max bounded onto the bed, startling a little shriek from her. Tony followed, carrying two cups of coffee. He smiled down at her as Max tried to sniff and lick her where she lay.

"Morning," Tony called to her as she tried to defend herself from the slobber. She had looked beautiful that morning when he woke with her, wrapped around her soft, smooth body. It had taken all his willpower to get out of bed to let Max out and make her a cup of coffee. "Max, down," he commanded, and Max obeyed.

"Morning," she replied warily. She narrowed her eyes at him, pulling the cover higher up her chest.

"Were you sniffing my pillow?" Chuckling, he put the two cups on the bedside table and sat next to her.

She blushed, colour rising from her chest "No," she scoffed.

He gave a knowing smile, so glad she didn't seem awkward with him after last night.

"I thought you would have gone by now," she told him, motioning for Max to join her back on the bed now he was a little calmer. He laid his chin on her chest, demanding she stroke the tufty hair on top of his head.

"Me too," Tony admitted, staring down at her, drinking her in. He had never spent a night with someone, had never wanted to.

"We made a deal: one night. It's not going to affect the relationship we had before." She was trying to appear confident and strong, but he heard the slight crack in her voice that told him she was putting on a front. "Don't feel obliged to stay."

"I don't," he replied.

"Good." She chewed her lip. "So why are you still here?"

"I don't know." He handed her a cup of coffee. "I just didn't want to leave yet."

She sipped the hot liquid, seeming to contemplate his words.

"Can I make you breakfast?" he asked, observing her intently as she nursed her cup close to her chest.

"Like I would ever refuse that offer," she laughed.

"That's all I'm good for then, is it?" He chuckled as he rose from the bed.

"Yep."

He drew in a sharp intake of breath. "Ooohhh. That hurts." Turning to leave with a smile on his face, he said, "Come down when you're ready, Sleeping Beauty." He left with Max at his heels.

In the kitchen, he gave Max his food and then busied himself with making breakfast, frying bacon, eggs and mushrooms, buttering bread and making more coffee. They needed it after last night. His groin tightened.

Just friends, that was it; it was all they could be. How they were going to manage it, he didn't know, but they had to. They'd had their night of pure pleasure, one night more than he could ever have thought he'd have with her.

When she entered the kitchen, he turned around and stopped where he stood, staring at her in her white dressing gown. The one from last night. He instantly reacted to the heavenly sight of her, the curve of her waist, her full breasts covered by a thin bit of material. She smiled to herself and deposited her empty cup in the sink next to him. He watched her, his tongue darting out to wet his lips.

"What?" she asked, her face straight, but a devilish twinkle in her eye.

"You know what," he replied. "That's how you want to play

it?" He raised one eyebrow. If he wasn't careful he would reach out and pull her to him, and lose himself in her.

"I have no idea what you're talking about." She turned to the table where her breakfast was waiting. As she retreated, he slapped her bum with a firm but playful smack. Damn it, he couldn't even last one minute.

"Ouch!" Giggling, she held her bum, protecting it from any more slaps.

"You're playing with fire!" he said. He didn't have to see the grin on her face to know how big it must be.

Plating up his breakfast, he joined her while she ate. How on earth were they meant to return to normal? How could he tame his desire for her now, when he knew what was under that dressing gown, when he knew how she tasted, when he knew what she sounded like when she shattered with his touch? *Shit, get your head in the game, Tony.*

"Did you sleep well?" she asked him.

"Surprisingly, yes."

"What do you mean, surprisingly?"

"I don't normally sleep with someone else in the room, do I? I thought you would have kept me up with your snoring, but I had the best night's sleep."

"I don't snore!" she said indignantly.

"I'm joking. Anyway, you might have done, I just didn't hear you."

She flicked his forehead. "Ow!" He held his hand over the spot, laughing. "What are you, five? Alright, I'm sure you don't snore, you sleep like a princess."

"Thank you."

He could see her brain whirring, questioning every look, every word, every act. She was going to drive herself crazy, drive them both crazy. He flicked her back.

"Ow!" She held her forehead, the tension breaking again.

They finished their breakfast in relative silence, with Max

163

enjoying his time outside. The back door was open, letting in a soft breeze, and the birds were chirping away. Tony felt lighter than he had done in weeks...months. That horrible nagging feeling was gone from his belly.

"What are your plans for today?" she asked as she cleared the table.

"I have to open up the pub today. I'll need to go soon, actually." He checked the time on his phone. He would give anything to not go in today, but John had covered so much for him recently, he didn't have a choice. The realisation that he wanted to spend the whole day with Jodie instead hit him like a ton of bricks.

She ran the water in the sink to do the washing up. "I was going to talk to you about work." She watched the soap suds foaming in the sink.

"Yeah?" He leant back against the draining board next to her, his arms crossed over his body, bracing himself.

"Can you not talk to anyone about last night, please?" she asked, busying herself with washing the dishes. "I don't want to become the talk of the town, or have people get the wrong impression."

"It's a village, actually," he joked with her. She splashed him with soap suds. "But no, of course I won't say anything to anyone. What happens between us, stays between us." He would have thought that was obvious.

"Thank you." She blew out her breath.

He stroked back a strand of her beautiful wavy hair that had fallen over her face. Unable to help himself, he tucked it behind her ear.

She shivered at his touch, the first intimate touch between them since last night.

"Jodie?" he mumbled.

"Yes," she replied, a little bit too loudly, scrubbing at a plate.

"Jodie?" he asked again, wanting her to look at him. He reached for her chin and directed her to look into his eyes. He traced her lower lip with his thumb, feeling electricity as he touched her.

"Yes?" she whispered back.

"Can I see you tonight?"

Her eyes widened in surprise. It took him by surprise too. He hadn't been planning on asking her, but he couldn't resist another night. Maybe one more would quench his desire for her?

She was still lost in his gaze and his caress. "Tonight?"

Pushing her back against the kitchen counter using her hips, he towered above her, looking down at her hooded eyes, her breath wispy against his face. "Tonight," he confirmed.

"But it was meant to be a one-night thing." Before she had finished her sentence, he lifted her up onto the kitchen counter and parted her legs so he could stand between them. He pushed himself further against her, unable to control himself.

"I want one more." He shouldn't be doing this, he knew that, but his body acted without him thinking.

"But you said—"

"I know what I said," he cut across her abruptly. "I've changed my mind. I want one more night." He rested his forehead against hers. "I just can't leave it at one night." She still didn't respond. "I know it's not fair to you," he whispered. "I know I'm being selfish. I just..." He sighed.

"One more night," she whispered.

He kissed her then, relief seeping from his body that had previously been tense with anticipation and guilt at what he was asking of her. He wasn't sure he would ever be able to resist kissing her again. "Thank you." Resting his forehead back on hers, he stood there for a while, just being with her.

Letting their bodies speak to each other where their owners couldn't.

Eventually, he lifted her back off the kitchen counter and took her place washing up. Being on his best behaviour, not wanting to jeopardise their agreement. She took the place next to him, drying up.

"Would you keep Max here for the day?" he asked her, looking out of the window at the little rascal chasing his tail in the garden.

"Of course," she replied happily.

"I'll walk him later on. He might get a bit restless, but he should be okay till I can get back."

"You don't like asking me to do things, do you?" she asked, staring at him intently.

He looked at her briefly. "Nope." He went back to his task.

"Well, I don't mind. So you shouldn't." She smiled then, seeming to relax a bit more.

Shortly after, Tony jumped in a quick bath and then left to open the pub. He didn't kiss her again, or even give her a hug. He just stood with his hands in his pockets, resisting the urge to pull her close, and said, "I'll see you soon, yeah?"

Then he turned his back on her and Max, unable to shake the feeling he was leaving a part of himself with them.

Maybe a happily ever after could be in his future?

CHAPTER 25

Max followed Jodie around as dutifully as ever, making sure that she didn't leave him like Tony had done. She tried to give him comfort and love, tried to ease his anxiety, but he didn't understand. Eventually trusting her enough to know that she wasn't going anywhere, he went to lie on his favourite sofa downstairs.

Sitting in her spare room on the floor, her business plans, portfolio and to-do lists spread out around her, she was feeling positive and motivated. Everything was going according to plan with Tony's house. She had a few small items to source to finish off the living room and then she could get started on the bedroom. Although she didn't know if she would be able to survive bed shopping with Tony. Sofa shopping had been enough of a test on her willpower, and now they had slept together, she might have to choose that piece online. There had also been a little bit of interest on her social media posts and she'd decided to respond to see if she could generate any firm leads.

Her phone rang, breaking her concentration. She smiled seeing Kelsie's name flash up on the screen.

"Hello," she answered, happy to be speaking with her friend. A lot had happened since they last spoke.

"How's it going?" Kelsie asked, concerned. "You seem very...chirpy?"

"I am very chirpy," Jodie chuckled, and filled Kelsie in on the news from the last few days.

"You're joking me, right?" Kelsie replied, stunned at the turn of events. "How much did you manage to cram into a couple of days?" Jodie never felt judged by Kelsie—that was one of the reasons they had always stayed so close. "I badgered Mark for all the details after he came to see you. He said he thought Tony might be described as 'hot stuff' but you know what he's like, he wouldn't give me enough information."

"Poor Mark." Jodie sympathised with him. She'd known he'd be in for an interrogation when he got home.

"Poor Mark?" she exclaimed. "Poor me, more like! I've had to wait days to be able to talk to you!" She chuckled, knowing full well she was being a pain in the arse.

"Anyway, Tony's coming back later on. I'm just sitting down working on the business."

"That's actually why I called," Kelsie told her. "I may have a lead for you."

"What?" Jodie replied, shocked. "Seriously?" She wanted to jump up and down for joy, but refrained before she got herself too excited. "Tell me more, tell me more."

"Well," Kelsie began, "I got to talking to a new lady at my spin class." Jodie shook her head in amazement at her friend's energy levels. "She said she works for a bespoke house builder and gave me her business card, obviously hoping I would buy one. So I then started talking to her about how they go about decorating the show homes. She said as they're a small company, they have only a handful of show homes and don't have an in-house team to do it. They contract the service out. Well, I immediately started to tell her about my amazing, brilliantly talented friend, who just started out on her own. Can I show her some pictures of the sort of stuff she creates? She said of course, probably more being friendly than anything. I showed her your posts on Instagram and I saw her eyes light up. I've got her here, I thought to myself. She asked me if these were all your designs and creations; you know what some people are like on Instagram? I told her of course, and she asked me to get you to call her. EEEEKKKK." She ended on a high-pitched shriek full of excitement. "How amazing is that?"

Jodie laughed at her friend's enthusiasm and skill for dramatic re-enactment. "You're kidding, right? That sounds incredible. And so unbelievable!"

"Would I ever lie to you? Of course I'm telling the truth! I'll send you a picture of her business card and you must ring her immediately, yes?"

"Yes, of course I will." Jodie breathed a sigh of relief. This could be amazing. "Thank you, Kelsie," she said sincerely. "I really appreciate everything you do for me. You're such a good friend. You realise we've spent the whole phone call talking about me?" She felt guilty for not returning the attention to Kelsie.

"Oh shut up! Your life is *way* more entertaining than mine at the moment. As and when my life turns interesting or I'm in need, I know you'll be there in a flash."

Jodie's heart swelled with love for this woman. They spoke a little while longer, just to catch up on Kelsie's life, before she insisted that Jodie hang up and ring the contact. She also demanded a text message later on to give her an update.

While Jodie waited for the text to come through from Kelsie, she ran downstairs to check Max was okay. He was sleeping soundly on the sofa. Knowing she would likely be a while on the phone, she opened the back door for him to come freely in and out if needed, and refilled his water bowl.

Then she went back upstairs to her 'office' to make the phone call to Louise. She shakily dialled her number and waited for her to pick up.

"Hello?" a voice came from the phone.

"Hi, is that Louise?"

"Speaking."

"Hi Louise, it's Jodie here. I got your number from Kelsie. She said to give you a call about some design work."

"Oh, yes." It obviously registered immediately, and Jodie was thrilled that Louise seemed genuinely interested in speaking to her. "I spoke with Kelsie and she showed me some of your portfolio. I then went home and looked through all of your social media accounts. I love your work and would really like to meet with you to talk about a possible collaboration."

Jodie stumbled for words, shocked at how easy that had been. "Ye-yes," she replied. "I would love that. Do you have any projects coming up?" She wanted to be sure how excited she could get.

"Quite a few as it so happens. We do have one designer, but he's trying to take a step back and branch into different areas. But we're expanding and have four new houses coming up shortly that need designing throughout. We would need to get going in the next couple of weeks really. Does that fit you?"

Jodie couldn't believe this turn of events. This could be career-making. Even though her tummy bubbled with excitement, she tried to remain professional. "Yes, that time frame fits me. We can set up a meeting if you like, and go through some initial ideas before I provide you with designs?"

"That sounds amazing. If you give me your email address, we can arrange a meeting. But sometime next week would be good. We would probably start off with two properties for now, as a trial, and all being well with the designs, go from there. Like I say, the company is expanding and my director has just told me he wants to get another four houses out by the end of the year. This could be a big contract."

"I'm sure I'll be able to fulfil all of your expectations, and I have the capacity to take on more projects in the future. Do you have a pen and paper for my email?" Jodie rattled off her address and they ended the call. She danced her way around the room in celebration, buzzing. She dropped Kelsie a text as promised, knowing she would be going on the school run any minute. And then she called her mum to explain the exciting new prospect she had picked up.

An hour after she called Louise, she went back downstairs to check on Max, expecting him to still be in the same place she'd left him.

Max wasn't sleeping on the sofa. So she checked the kitchen, and then the back garden, but still couldn't see him. She called his name and listened for the tip-tapping of his paws. Nothing. "Max," she called again, climbing the stairs to see if he had slipped into her room. It was empty.

Panic started to rise in her. "Max," she shouted, more urgently this time. Running back downstairs, she checked under the coffee table and the kitchen table, then went back out into the garden.

"Max," she called desperately. "Here boy, do you want a treat?" That would get him going. He must be in a bush, or maybe he'd managed to get into the shed. She wrenched the door open, noting it had been firmly shut. He couldn't possibly have gotten in.

"Max, come on boy. Walkies." She crouched down, peering through all the bushes. *Please, please, please*. She urged him out of wherever he was hiding. As she straightened once more, she looked out over the fields at the back of the house, clocking the half fence that separated her garden from the fields beyond.

Shit. Tears welled in her eyes and her throat burnt. She

sprinted to the gate. "Max," she called out, fumbling with the bolt. She looked this way and that, desperately trying to spot some form of brown in the greens and yellows that stretched out before her. "Max," she bellowed.

Her heart sank. If he hadn't come to her calls yet, he was either out of earshot or unable to return. Grabbing her phone from her back pocket, she dialled the one number she was dreading, her fingers trembling.

Closing the gate behind her, she walked further into the field, searching for Max while she waited for Tony to answer.

"Hello?" he answered, happy and bright. She could have collapsed in a heap.

"Tony?" she said shakily. How could she tell him, where could she even begin?

"What's happened?" His panic was immediate.

"It's M-Max," she spluttered, trying to control her tears long enough to get the news out. They needed to act quickly. "I've lost him."

"What do you mean, you've lost him?" he shouted.

She winced. "I'm so sorry, I think he must have jumped my back gate when I was on a call. I'm trying to find him, but I need you to come help me," she sobbed.

"You're sure he's not in the house?"

"I've searched everywhere. He isn't coming when I call him and I can't see him anywhere," she rambled.

"I'm coming now."

"I'm in the middle of the field at the back of my house."

"I'll run around. Find him, Jodie!" He hung up the phone.

Through her tears, Jodie carried on calling Max's name.

CHAPTER 26

Tony's heart beat against his ribs, thundering to the sound of his feet on the pavement. He had never run so fast in his life. He'd quickly shouted to Micha to man the bar and sprinted out of the pub, not caring what anyone thought.

How could this have happened? *Shit*. He'd left Max again. He'd thought Max would have been happy with Jodie there, but he must have been so hurt about the other night, when Tony had left him on his own, that he panicked.

Racing along to the field behind Jodie's house, Tony desperately hoped she had found him already. He couldn't bear to lose Max. He was the only living thing he'd cared about, until Jodie had come along. He shook his head to rid himself of any thoughts apart from Max. He was all that mattered.

"Any luck?" he shouted to Jodie before he even reached her. Dread filled him up as he saw no Max with her. All she could do was shake her head. "Shit!" He ran his hands through his already tousled hair. "You're absolutely sure he isn't in the house?" He was clutching at straws.

"Check if you like," she said, handing him her bundle of keys. "I'll keep searching out here."

He saw the tear marks on her cheeks, her red eyes, her flushed skin. But he couldn't comfort her while his own heart was breaking into a million pieces. He ran through the house, calling for Max, hoping he was curled up in a corner or under a blanket. Nothing. *Fuck, he really was gone.*

"We need to split up and look for him strategically," he told Jodie when he returned from searching the house, trying to be calm. He couldn't even look her in the eye. He held out her keys for her to take. "I'm going to text Micha so she can tell the locals. They can start looking around the green and village. He's probably gone to places he knows, trying to find me." Agony seared every part of his body. How could this have happened?

"Where should I look?" Jodie asked, her voice shaking.

She hadn't protected the thing he loved the most. *She* was the reason this had happened. He shot her a look, and she recoiled. Taking a steadying breath, he looked away again and said, "You remember that walk you met us on? Go there. Take the opening we came out of and follow it through the woods to a stream. You'll be able to see the path, we've walked it so many times. I'm going in the other direction—there's another walk we take there." He started walking away. "Text me every fifteen minutes if there's no sign of him, and ring me if you find him."

Then he ran across the field without looking back, trying to text Micha as he ran, hoping that Max had had the good sense to stick to one of their walks or go to the pub. Perhaps he'd been sniffing in a bush when Tony ran past him.

Max couldn't be gone. It just couldn't happen.

CHAPTER 27

Jodie started walking, trying to get her bearings and remember the way. She'd had the common sense to put her trainers on when she first tried to find Max in the garden, and grab her house and car keys as a just-in-case.

How could this have happened? Why on earth did she leave the back door open? She should have just woken Max up, let him out and brought him back in before making her phone call. It could have waited for ten minutes.

Poor Max. What must have gone through his mind? He had probably woken up and wondered where she'd gone, and thought she had left him too. Her heart ached. He probably jumped the fence in panic, wanting to find Tony to feel safe again.

But then what had happened? He could have wandered for miles by now, or someone could have taken him. What if he was hurt? Fear made her step her pace up, calling Max's name as she walked.

Finally reaching the place Tony had described, she walked through the bushes. Although she could clearly see the path Tony and Max would regularly take, it was still dark and matted with weeds and overgrown bushes and plants. Stomping her way through it all, nettles and brambles snagging on her legs and arms, she searched for any sign of Max. She continued calling his name but was met with deadly silence.

The path started to dwindle. If she lost it now, she had no hope of finding it again. She checked her phone and tried to text Tony the fifteen-minute update, but she had no signal. Sighing, she replaced her phone in her pocket. He would be furious when he didn't get the update…well, more furious than he already was. But there wasn't anything she could do about it now. That look he'd given her would haunt her forever. The pure disgust. She shook herself. There wasn't time to worry about that now. *Only think about Max.*

The path grew wilder and darker the further she walked. She carried on trudging, determined to make it to the stream. *Please let me find him.*

Just a little way ahead of her, a clearing appeared. Small streaks of light shone through from the trees, and the faintest trickling sounded from the stream. "Max?" she shouted again, her voice echoing around her. Straining her ears to catch the tiniest sound that may mean Max was there, she carried on forward. "Max?" Small, sharp, rocks were strewn along the stream's edge, and smoother pebbles lay under the bubbling water. A steep hill rose on the other side, crumbling mud and stone visible from years of exposure. It was a beautiful, peaceful place, but at this very moment it filled her with dread. If Max had come here in a panic, running around like a maniac, he could easily have hurt himself.

"Max!" she bellowed, looking up and down the stream. At last she heard something. Her heart pounded. "Max?" she called, looking to her right and heading in the direction of the sound. It had sounded like an animal, but it was so faint she couldn't be sure. Then the sound came again. What was it?

Yelping. It must be Max. She broke into a run, trying to keep her footing on the slippery rocks and pebbles underneath. "I'm coming, Max." Where could he be?

The stream dropped away abruptly, as if the land had slipped a long time ago to create the tiniest waterfall. Yet it must still have been at least a six-foot drop, with tree roots, brambles and rocks at the bottom.

Scanning the foot of the waterfall for Max, she called for him again. Then, finally, movement.

Max lay on his side at the edge of the water, staring up at her, not moving apart from his tail flicking slightly at the sight of her.

"Oh, Max! Stay where you are."

He wasn't moving—he must be hurt. She scanned the scenery for a way down. Both sides of the stream were quite steep, but the slightly safer route to take was off to the left. She moved as quickly and safely as she could. If she twisted her ankle, she would be no use to Max.

As she wound her way towards him, she slipped on the rocks, falling a few times. She protected herself by sticking out her hands, but the sharp rocks cut her palms and arms, blood appearing instantly.

Max watched her every step, her every fall, yelping and howling for her help. He must have run off of the ledge and hurt himself on the landing, probably too panicked to even think about the jump.

Eventually, she reached him. Kneeling by his side, she stroked him gently, offering words of comfort. "I'm here boy, I'm so sorry." Tears spilled onto her cheeks. Max shivered, his fur wet from the stream. How long had he been lying here like this?

Running her hands gently down his wet, shivering body to find where he was hurt, her hands shook as much as he did. He held out his back leg, whimpering when she put the faintest touch on it. For all she knew it could be sprained, or worse, broken. But either way, he wouldn't be able to walk on it. He needed a vet.

"Alright boy, I'm going to call Daddy." She kissed his head, and he licked her face, panting heavily. She pulled her phone out. Still no signal. "Shit, shit, shit. Right, what the fuck are we going to do?" *Think, damn it.*

There was no other way—she'd have to try to carry him back. He was just about the right length for her to carry him in two arms. His weight might be a problem though. She bit her lip. Would she be able to carry him the whole way back? Her arms would probably give out.

But there wasn't another option. She would have to bear his weight—she couldn't just leave him here to go back and find help.

Scanning the area, she tried to find their best escape route. They'd have to cut across the stream and then hope to find a smaller slope to walk up and get back onto the path. If she could find it again.

She moved around to Max's back, and scooped him up in her arms. He yelped. "Shhh boy, it's okay. I've got you." He wasn't too heavy at the moment, but she'd soon start to feel the burn. She moved as quickly as she could without slipping on the ground beneath her, and Max rested his head over her arm, whining quietly.

They came to a place where she could walk up the slope and rejoin the path. The tugging in her biceps was now creeping to her forearms. Even her hands hurt. *Come on, you can do this.*

By some luck of God, she was able to retrace her steps, branches and thorns snagging at her skin and clothes. They soon came to the spot where the woodland gave way to the fields behind her house. Her arms were lead weights, grazed and cut, sweat trickled down her back, and her throat was on fire from her heaving breaths. *Just a little bit further.*

The houses grew bigger as she neared them. Just a few more minutes and she would make it to her car. Her thighs objected to every step, feeling as if they were about to rip open.

"Tony?" she cried out with all her might. *Please let him have come to find them.* At any moment she was sure she would drop Max. "Tony?" she shouted through her tears. *Please take Max.* Her arms couldn't take it anymore. She had to put him down. But she would never be able to pick him up again. "Tony, please?" Max howled with her. Her chest seared with every ragged breath she took as she somehow managed to keep walking, her arms trembling.

She carried on pushing, her car finally visible. Her arms bounced up and down from the lactic acid circling her body. Her legs turned to jelly. *Thirty more seconds. Just thirty more seconds.*

At last. She placed Max on the ground, careful not to drop him and hurt him further, she fumbled with her keys and opened the car, her fingers trembling on the button. She cleared the mess from the back seats, swiping it all into the footwells, and laid her emergency blanket out on the seat for him. Then she gently lifted him into the car, her arms and legs immediately smarting at the movement. Max yelped.

"Shhh boy, you'll be okay. I'm sorry," she sobbed, wrapping him in the blanket.

Shutting the door, thankful the bright spring sunshine had warmed it up, she got into the driver's seat and googled the nearest vet practice. Her hands shook on the steering wheel, waiting for the directions to appear. "Ten minutes away," she shouted back to Max as she raced out of the village as directed.

She hit the call button on her steering wheel. "Ring Tony,"

she demanded. The dialling tones were harsh against her ears. The call didn't connect.

Try again in a minute.

She only lasted twenty seconds.

"Call Tony!" she commanded. Again the dialling tones sounded, then stopped. Perhaps he didn't have any signal either? She bit her lip. As the satnav directed her this way and that she tried Tony again, and after the third ring he picked up.

"Jodie, tell me you found him." His voice shook as though he was crying.

"I have him. He's hurt and we're on our way to the nearest vets now," she blurted. "Run to your car and meet me there."

"What do you mean, he's hurt?" Wind rushed through the phone.

"I found him at the bottom of the drop at the stream. He's wet and his leg is hurt. I don't know if it's broken, or sprained. I'm almost at the vets."

"Why didn't you text or call me?" he demanded.

She saw red. "I did!" she shouted back at him. "I texted like you asked and this is the third call. I had no signal for the text to go through."

Silence. Before she could even say another word, Tony hung up.

She made it to the vets five minutes later. She eased Max out of the back seat as gently as possible, then pushed her way through the front doors into the veterinary practice.

"Help," she called before the door had even closed behind her. "My dog has had an accident and hurt his leg. I think he jumped down into a stream and hurt himself. He's wet and cold." The words tumbled out at the poor receptionist, who stared in bewilderment at her. "Please help me!" she pleaded. "He's been hurt for more than an hour."

As the receptionist stood up, one of the doors opened and

a man in a white shirt with rolled-up sleeves came out. "What's happened?" he asked, striding over to Jody and Max in a few steps. He took a light pen from his shirt pocket and shone it in Max's eyes.

"His leg is hurt. It's an emergency."

"Bring him through," he told her and held the door open so she could lay Max on the examination table. He apologised to the people waiting, but they seemed to murmur in agreement that they could wait for an emergency.

"Right," the vet said, closing the door behind him. "Tell me everything from the beginning." He checked Max over as she spoke. He was a handsome man, well built and dark. He had caring eyes and his arms were strong beneath his shirt. There was something familiar about him. But Jodie shook her head, she only cared about Max.

She told the vet everything—how Max had gone missing, where she found him, the state he was in and how long he could have been hurt for. She told him how she'd carried him, trying not to inflict any further damage, admitting he had yelped a few times, but she couldn't just leave him there to go and find help.

Eventually, the vet looked up. "Now you said this was your dog, but I know Max, and I know Max's owner, and you are not him." He raised an eyebrow sternly.

She blushed and explained. "I just said that for quickness. I was looking after Max while Tony was working. I called Tony as soon as I knew he'd gone missing and we split up looking for him. I just happened to find him first, and I've already called Tony to come here. He should be here any minute."

He considered her for a moment, then nodded. "Okay. We need to get him x-rayed and warmed up. We have a private waiting room which I'll show you to. You understand that I have to call Tony to tell him Max is here? If he doesn't corroborate your story, I'll have to call the police. I can't give

181

you any information on Max as you are not his owner. Do you understand?"

She nodded her head, feeling like a criminal. He strode to the other door behind her and called for someone to show her to the waiting room and for a nurse to help move Max. Jodie bent her head over Max's ear and gave him a kiss, whispering again that she was sorry and he was going to be okay.

Max just lay still, panting and shivering.

CHAPTER 28

James was a good guy, Tony knew that. But right now, he wanted to punch him in the face. He was refusing to let him see Max.

Tony had driven like a mad man to get there, hoping that Jodie hadn't gotten lost on the way or gone to a different vet practice. James had been waiting for him in the car park, telling him to calm down and that Max was in the best place possible.

Couldn't he see that the best place for Max was with Tony?

James had told him how Jodie brought Max in, her arms shaking and cut to ribbons. How she had found him, shivering and cold, and carried him all the way to the car. That she had done the right thing, at every point in time. Tony scoffed. He didn't want to hear her name.

"Tony," James scolded him. "Don't be so ignorant to think that this couldn't have happened if he was with you. We're all human, we all make mistakes. She's beating herself up about it badly enough without you being an arsehole too!"

Tony sank onto the pavement, his head in his hands,

leaning over his knees. "Fuck!" he yelled out into the quietness. James sat next to him, patting him on the back.

"He's in the best place, mate. You know we'll take care of him. He's on a drip and under sedation so that we can x-ray him. He might need surgery."

Tony's eyes filled with tears. They toppled out and fell onto the cracked tarmac. He just sat. Silent. Taking it all in.

"I'm guessing this Jodie means something to you?" James asked. Tony didn't respond. His heart stung at her betrayal. "She hasn't done anything wrong, Tony. Don't punish her for this. You'll regret it."

Tony scoffed again. "Coming from Casanova himself, yeah?" He couldn't believe he was being lectured by James. About women of all things. He was as clueless about relationships as Tony was.

"Yeah, I know. But I can tell something is going on. You don't leave Max with anyone, so she must be special. Just hear her out, okay?"

"Just go and fix Max, will you?" Tony bit at him.

"Let me get you to the waiting room and I'll check on him. The x-ray should be done now." James stood up from the pavement and Tony followed.

He walked into the private waiting room where Jodie sat, staring at the blank wall. Her clothes were stained with mud, her hair a tangled mess, and there were red scratches and dried blood all up her arms. He turned away, unable to look at her.

"Have you spoken to the vet?" she asked quietly, her voice raspy. His heart stung as he nodded. "And? What's happening?"

"He's pretty sure it's a broken leg. There's a deep gash too. It depends what the x-ray shows, but it could be surgery." Tony slumped into a chair, eyes closed.

The air vibrated around him with her energy. The smell of

her shampoo and body wash mixed with mud and blood wrapped itself around him, clinging to every fibre on his clothes. She touched his shoulder, her hand burning into him.

"I'm so sorry, Tony," she whispered.

He flinched from her touch. "What good is sorry going to do? Is it going to turn back time?" He sprang up from the chair and paced the little room, his hands gripping his hips, trying to control his emotions. "I trusted you. Max trusted you."

"Tony," she said.

He could barely look at her. "I don't want to hear it."

"But—"

James walked in and looked between them, sizing up the situation. He went over to Tony and placed a hand on his back.

"Tony, it's not Jodie's fault. Can't you see she feels bad enough?" James looked at her with sympathy in his eyes. "And being angry isn't going to make Max better. Come on, we talked about this." Tony felt his friend's calmness washed over him as James guided him to a chair. "She cares for Max very much, that's obvious. She carried him all the way to her car and did the best thing for him. You should be thanking her." James sat next to him. "Now, I have news."

"I'll leave you to it," Jodie said, and slipped from the room, silently closing the door behind her.

Tony felt like all the air had been sucked from the room. He stared at the door, long and hard, while James gave him the news.

CHAPTER 29

The day after Max's accident, Jodie was preparing the house for her mum and Kelsie to come round. After she called them, sobbing and telling them what had happened, they had both dropped their plans and arranged a last-minute trip to see her.

Thankfully Jodie had already booked in a couple of days off from The Dog, just so that she could concentrate on the business. But now she would be using those days to hide and wallow away the days. Her dining table was full of pictures of Tony and Max, his parents and friends from the pub. She had taken them to place in matching frames that she would hang on the walls and on the bespoke bookshelves she had commissioned. Every time she looked at them, her heart seared in pain again, so she'd had to take them upstairs to her office and cover them with a spare sheet.

She desperately needed to see her mum and Kelsie. She hadn't seen them in so long, her heart ached for them. Being around them would do her good, recentering her on what mattered in her life.

She surveyed her newly-finished living room with pride. It

had taken her a while but she was finally happy with how it had turned out.

Car doors slammed outside. She peeked out of the window. Sure enough, it was Kelsie's SUV, and her mum and Kelsie were straightening their clothes, looking around the village green. It was the first time either had visited her. Kelsie was always so busy 'mumming' and Sandra had been away for three weeks on a long-awaited cruise. It was a shame her dad was unable to make it, but it was a weekday and it was surprising enough that her mother had been able to get away from her office.

Jodie ran to the door to welcome them in, hugging them both so tightly, glad to finally have them there. When Kelsie had phoned her back last night to say she'd organised with Sandra to come down today, Jodie had tried to stop them. She was fine, seriously, she must just be hormonal and tired. But that lie hadn't stopped either of them. They had insisted they were turning up, so she had better have some biscuits in. Now they were here, she was so glad that they'd come. She didn't know how much she needed to see them until this very moment.

Eventually, she released them and showed them into her cottage where they made the correct 'oohing' and 'ahhing' sounds at her living room.

Her mother hugged her and said, "It's perfect, Jodie." She had tears in her green eyes, her blonde hair glistening and sleek. "This is exactly what you needed. I'm so proud of you."

Kelsie hugged her too. "You never know, maybe Mark and I could move here. Mark loved it when he came to visit and he always talks about moving to somewhere quiet and peaceful."

Nothing would make Jodie happier.

She gave them a tour of the house before returning to make the cups of tea. They sat in her living room, drinking and catching up, nibbling on the biscuits that Jodie had run to get from the corner shop that morning.

"Your dad is going to love it here," Sandra told her. "We've put a date in the diary for next weekend to come down again, if you're free?"

Jodie put it in her calendar but was sure she wouldn't have anything else on.

"So…" Sandra began, her tone of voice changing. Jodie's heart started to beat a little faster—she knew what was coming. "How are you feeling after yesterday?" Her mum laid a reassuring hand on her knee.

"Dreadful," Jodie replied. It was no use trying to hide it from these two. Together they could sniff out any secret like a bloodhound. "I feel so guilty."

"I told you last night you shouldn't!" Kelsie said.

"Kelsie," Sandra replied, her chunky necklaces banging together as she turned to Jodie's friend. "She feels how she feels; we can't change that. But perhaps we can give her a little comfort and support."

Kelsie sighed and Sandra turned back to her daughter.

"I understand that I shouldn't feel guilty," Jodie said. "I know I didn't do anything on purpose, and I'd change it if I could. But I still feel dreadful about it."

Her mum nodded. "It's still early days yet, I'm sure that will change with time. Have you had an update on how Max is?"

Jodie shook her head. She hadn't heard anything from Tony, not even a text message to say if Max had had surgery or not.

"I'm sure he's fine," Kelsie said, fiddling with her own necklace that had Maisie's name on it.

"Whose dog is it?" Sandra asked.

Jodie had kept the details quite vague yesterday, not wanting to divulge her feelings. "Tony's," she replied.

"As in Tony, your boss and your first client?"

"Yes." Jodie looked down at her hands. "Max is adorable and they're the only friends I've really made here so far. Everyone's lovely here, but they're more like acquaintances at the moment." And now she had lost it all.

"Why don't we go for a walk and you can show us around?" Sandra suggested. "It doesn't do any good moping about, and a bit of fresh air will clear your head." She rose from the sofa and straightened her flowy top.

That was the last thing Jodie wanted to do. "Mum," she pleaded. "I don't fancy a walk, and the village is so tiny there aren't really any sights to see."

"Well, the pub then?" she said, looking out of the window. Jodie exchanged a quick pleading look with Kelsie. That would be even worse. What if Tony was there? Unfortunately her mum turned round and caught them making faces at each other. "What?" she demanded.

"I don't want to go there," Jodie replied, feeling like she was five again, being a brat.

"Why?"

Jodie sighed heavily. She didn't have the energy to come up with an excuse, so she went with the truth. "I don't want to bump into Tony. He was devastated when I told him what had happened. He blames me. He won't want to see me."

Sandra was silent for a moment. "I understand how he could be very upset with the situation. But I'm sure he'll come round with some time to think and knowing that Max is going to be okay. Whenever you talk about him, he sounds like a reasonable, nice, caring man."

"He is a nice, caring man. But I don't think reason will come into it. He loves Max more than anything, and he doesn't let people in and he certainly doesn't trust them very easily. I broke his trust and that led to Max being hurt. He's really angry."

"Oh, come on now. He'll see that you care for Max, and how deeply sorry you are. His anger would be gone by now."

Jodie shook her head. "I can't, Mum."

"Nonsense. He's a businessman. He won't have an argument with a customer and an employee in his place of business. He has a reputation to think about."

"Well, he took a date there," Jodie mumbled, and immediately regretted it. Sandra's eyes lit with understanding.

"Ahh. You have feelings for him?" she asked. "That makes a lot more sense now. Why didn't you tell me in the first place?" She sat next to Jodie again, taking her hands in hers.

"I don't," she mumbled.

Kelsie scoffed, and Jodie shot her a look.

"Well, seriously?" Kelsie tried to defend herself. "It's obvious you do."

"Does he like you back?" Sandra asked her.

"Well not now!" Jodie retorted.

Sandra cuddled her. "Times like these will make or break people, Jodie," she told her daughter, rubbing her back. "If it's meant to be, he'll come around and apologise for how he's behaved, and you'll apologise again for losing Max. If it isn't meant to be, then it's best to end now, before you get too hurt."

Jodie nodded. She knew her mum was right. It didn't make it any easier though.

"Right!" Sandra said, her overly cheerful tone making Jodie and Kelsie jump. "Pull your big girl pants up, Jodie, and show us to that pub. I'm dying for a glass of wine! He won't even be there anyway, I bet. If he loves Max as much as you say he does, then he'll either be at home with him or at the vet's."

Kelsie jumped up too, in a show of support for Sandra. Jodie groaned. Maybe she should have insisted harder that they didn't come today?

Kelsie pushed her up the stairs, demanding that she get

changed. If Tony was at the pub, she needed to look 'banging'. Thankfully, her mum didn't catch the cheeky wink Kelsie sent her way. She put on a smart pair of jeans, some ankle boots with a low chunky heel, and a white top. She applied a little extra blush to her blanched cheeks and went over her mascara.

"Right, let's go then," she shouted down to them as she went down the stairs.

They walked the short distance to the pub, Jodie staying quiet as her mum and Kelsie chatted away. When they walked past Tony's house, she ducked her head. His car was there but she didn't dare look inside.

Jodie pushed upon the heavy door and let her mum and Kelsie through. John greeted them at the bar, and Jodie introduced them all. As he poured out their drinks, John bent low to Jodie and said, "I heard about Max. How are you feeling? Still shook up?" Jodie nodded. "He'll be alright," he said, flinging his beloved tea towel over his shoulder.

"Have you heard from Tony?" She couldn't help but ask.

John nodded, compassion in his eyes. Why was she so transparent? "He just said he'd need to be covered for the next few days so he can look after Max." Jodie bit her lip. "Look, I've known Tony a long time. Just give him time, okay? He'll come round." She nodded again and John left to serve another customer.

They took their drinks to a table, chatting away. The more they talked, the more relaxed Jodie felt, forgetting about all her worries.

"So what's happening with your work now?" Kelsie asked Jodie, sipping her lemonade.

"Well, I booked in a meeting with Louise next week. And then I was meant to be finishing Tony's living room this week and starting his bedroom too. But..." She shrugged, not knowing what would happen now.

"When are you meant to be going there?" Sandra asked.

"Tomorrow. That's what we had arranged prior to yesterday."

"Has he told you not to come?"

"No, he hasn't spoken to me, has he?"

"Then I say, if he doesn't tell you not to go, that you head over tomorrow as planned and ask him if he wants you to continue," Kelsie told her. Sandra agreed.

Jodie pulled a cheesy chip from the plate they had ordered, thinking. Tomorrow was bound to be a disaster.

CHAPTER 30

Ding dong.

Tony had been dreading this exact moment. All morning he'd been on edge, unable to sit still. Waiting.

Opening the door to Jodie, his hands shook.

"Hi," she croaked, her throat apparently as dry as his. He couldn't even manage to say hello back, so he just nodded to her. At the sound of her voice, Max started crying from the kitchen. Tony had shut him away so he wouldn't get excited seeing her. Damn him for loving her so much.

"I just came to remind you the sofa and armchair will be delivered at nine today."

"Yes, I remembered that," he said calmly. Damn her for looking so gorgeous today. Her hair was pulled back into a ponytail, her green eyes shining bright with anticipation.

"And I was due to come and finish the living room today." She nibbled at her lip.

"Yes, I remembered that too." He didn't move a muscle.

"Do you still want me to continue?"

"Yes, that was the arrangement."

She winced ever so slightly, a blush spreading across her

cheeks. He knew it would travel across her chest as well. Why did this woman have such an effect on him?

"I didn't bring my stuff with me, so I can go and grab it, if you're happy for me to work today?"

"That's fine."

He could see an argument raging inside of her. She probably wanted to scream at him for being so cold. But the fight had gone out of her. He had done that.

"Okay. I'll be back in a minute."

She turned away from him and he felt a sudden surge of panic at her leaving. He forced himself to stay put. It was better this way. They had gotten too close and look what had happened. He wasn't destined for a happily ever after with someone, and he had no doubt in his mind that she deserved one. Even if that meant she would spend her life with someone else. His heart tugged at the thought.

He left the door on the latch and retreated to Max, who was still lying in his bed where Tony had left him, his face sad and tired. His leg had been shaved and bandaged up following his surgery. James had successfully pinned his bones and he was on a course of antibiotics to ward off any infection.

Clattering and thuds sounded from the living room and Max lifted his head, whimpering. He was longing to see Jodie. But he didn't move. Tony sat on the floor with him, taking off the stupid cone now that he was with him and could make sure he didn't nibble at his leg.

Max dropped his head onto Tony's lap, as if also succumbing to their fate of being lonely forever. Tony scratched his ears, trying to comfort him, knowing it wouldn't help. He wanted Jodie, just like Tony had wanted her when he sat in the waiting room when Max was in surgery.

He had been left alone in that room, like in a prison. And he had waited for hours. All he could do was wish Jodie was with him, holding his hand, resting her head on his shoulder.

Just being with him at the worst moment of his life. But she wasn't, because he had pushed her away.

Damn himself, for being such an arsehole.

The kitchen door was still closed. Max whimpered from behind the door again and Jodie's heart broke. She was being shut out, but she just had to deal with it.

Surveying the room, she noted the last-minute touch ups of painting she had to do. The sofa would arrive soon, then she just had to stage everything.

Jodie couldn't help but smile thinking about Tony's reaction to the sofa that day. It felt like a lifetime ago, so much had happened since then. But she had known right away that he had found the right sofa; of course it had to be the last of the bunch. He had seemed so relaxed as soon as he sat down. And even though she had tried to ban herself from touching him again following their near kiss, she hadn't been able to stop herself and went to cuddle up next to him. She didn't know how long they'd sat there for, but eventually a sales guy walked over to them and Tony didn't hesitate to put his order through. While he was confirming the delivery details, she had wandered through the store, found the perfect armchair for Max, and added that to the order too.

Now she moved Max's old armchair and the small sofa on her own, nearer to the front door, in order for the delivery guys to dispose of them. Thankfully they were small and lightweight, as it looked like Tony would never be seen again.

Her heart stung, thinking that gone were the days he'd cared for her and helped her out, being chivalrous. Was it because of Max? Or maybe it was because he'd had his way with her, got what he wanted, and she was no longer needed. She felt dirty, like a discarded dog toy. Maybe Max's accident had come at the perfect time for him to use it as an excuse and hide the real reason from her.

"Hello," a man shouted at the front door, breaking her from her thoughts. "Sofa delivery."

"Hi." She joined him to check over the delivery. Then, stepping to one side so they could move the armchair and sofa, she watched them work. What a miserable day.

Seeing the sofa and new armchair sitting in their correct places, she felt a surge of pride. They were perfect. The corner sofa sat against the back wall next to the kitchen. It was a deep brown leather but was sleek and minimal in design. A few cushions and a perfectly placed throw would give it some warmth. Not too much, as it was a bachelor pad after all. Max's new chair was a grey wingback armchair. It was quite large, but would sit perfectly next to the window and allow Max to doze to his heart's content.

Tony's new coffee table had already been delivered and she now dragged this to its rightful place. It was a rustic rectangular piece—the wood on top was uneven, rough and dark, and matched the wood in the new shelving units exactly. The base was a dark steel. She placed it on top of a rug that she'd bought to ensure the expanse of wood wasn't too much, and because Tony had seemed to love the idea of lying down in front of the fire.

She sighed again. She had kidded herself then to think maybe they'd do that together one day.

Max started whining again and the kitchen door opened. "Max, stay back," Tony instructed, sliding through the smallest sliver of opening possible. She was obviously so untrustworthy, she wouldn't even be allowed to see Max.

"Wow," Tony exclaimed looking around the room. "This looks great."

He actually smiled. Now his face had softened, just a touch, Jodie noticed the dark circles under his red eyes and his tousled hair. His usual stubble was slightly longer than normal. He wore his jogging bottoms and a t-shirt, and his feet were bare.

"It's not finished yet," she told him. There were still a few hours of work yet to get it exactly how it should be, with books on the shelves and the photos she had reframed. There were some perfect ones of Max. He barked at her voice in frustration, as if he knew she was thinking about him.

"Please let me see him," she asked quietly. Tony looked between her and the kitchen, thinking. "Please, Tony, you haven't even told me what happened to him or how he is." She took a step towards him, holding her hand out as if to touch him, to offer some comfort.

He recoiled from her. "You haven't asked."

"That's because you blame me. You can't even look me in the eye, you're so angry at me."

He shook his head. She saw worry cross his face, his eyebrows furrowed. He looked like a father contemplating the best course of action for his child. She could feel the love and concern seeping from his body.

And then she realised. It wasn't anger that Tony felt, it was worry. Max was his everything, his whole world, his trusty companion, and he had been fraught with worry that he would lose him. And then what? How would he have ever coped with that?

She understood now. It wasn't her that he hated, he was just trying to protect Max…and himself. She saw him through new eyes. "I'll keep low and try to not get him excited," she promised, when he still hadn't replied.

He thought for a moment. "Okay," he said reluctantly.

He hadn't given in lightly, and this was the first step of her regaining his trust. Hopefully.

She sank to the floor as Tony opened the door and gripped Max's collar tightly so he didn't rush to her and hurt himself.

Max had a large cone on and he dragged his bandaged leg behind him. Jodie wanted to shout "hello" and tickle him all over. She was so excited to see him, but she managed to refrain and not say a word until he was next to her. Her heart broke looking into his eyes. He seemed just as tired as Tony did. He was skinnier too, and his fur wasn't as soft or silky as it normally was.

She kissed him on the nose, which earnt her a lick on the cheek. Whispering softly to him, she shushed him to calm him down. His tail wiggled in excitement but he managed to stay still. Sort of.

"What happened?" She looked up at Tony, who was staring down at them. Was she imagining it or was there the slightest smile on his lips, a little gleam in his eye?

~

Tony tucked his hands in his pockets. Jodie didn't look away from him as he filled her in. "He had to have plates to fix his broken leg together, but he's healthy and the surgery went well. They let me take him home yesterday. James drinks at the pub regularly and said he would stop in to check on him. I have to keep him calm and rested."

"I have a surprise for you, Max," Jodie whispered. She took the lead from Tony, their hands grazing ever so slightly, and led Max over to his new armchair. His bum grew wigglier as he sniffed the new chair.

"He can't jump up!" Tony told her, suddenly gripped with fear that he might hurt himself.

"I know," she said calmly, picking Max up. He was too big for her to carry—he looked awkward in her arms, and her muscles strained. Yet she gently laid him on the chair without touching his leg, and he didn't even whimper. There were still faint cuts and bruises along her arms from that day, and Tony seared with guilt. She must have been hurt too. She had carried Max, like that, all the way to her car. She must have been exhausted.

Now Max tried to sniff the chair, but his cone prevented him. Jodie undid it and placed it on the floor next to her. Max laid his head down, lovingly staring up at her as she stroked him. It wasn't long before he closed his eyes. She smiled like a proud mum getting her precious newborn baby to sleep on their own. She reached round for the blanket she had discarded on the floor, not taking her eyes from Max.

Tony handed her the blanket, their hands touching again for the briefest second. He felt the zing spark between them as they touched, and heard her sharp intake of breath, knowing she felt what he felt too. Yet she still didn't look away from Max.

Laying the blanket over him, she tucked him in like a baby and continued stroking his tufty head with her thumb.

"Do you want a coffee?" Tony whispered. He hadn't even offered her a drink since she had been here. His gut wrenched at his behaviour.

"Yes please," she nodded, smiling up at him, relief showing on her face.

Tony made her a coffee and sat with his laptop on his new sofa while she tiptoed around, finishing her last few tasks. The sofa was perfect. Just the right size for the space and so comfortable. He had his feet up, relaxing for the first time in his home…ever.

He had an email from his mum, entitled 'Look what I just found.' He opened it up. *I've just been going through some of our old pictures we had scanned onto the computer. How cute you were. Love Mum. X*

He opened up the attachments. The first was a picture of him all bundled up in blankets, his dad holding him and staring at him intently. He could have only been a few weeks old. His mum sat next to his dad smiling up at the camera, tiredness in her eyes, but looking so happy. In the next picture he was sitting in an old-fashioned high chair, food smeared all around his mouth. His dad was feeding him and laughing at the mess he was making. Tony hadn't seen these photos before, of his dad happy with his family.

The next was Tony playing on a blanket outside at his nan's house. He must have been a year old. His mum and dad sat in the background. He zoomed in on them. They were cuddling together, smiling, looking at each other with love in their eyes. He zoomed in further. He had never seen this picture before. Never seen them smiling with love at each other. He was transfixed. So at some point they had loved each other. What had changed?

He logged onto Facebook, something he very rarely went on, and found his mum's profile. Her recent holiday pictures had gone up, and he searched through them. There were lots of pictures of his mum or his dad smiling at the camera, holding a glass of wine at a dinner table. But then he found what he wanted. A picture of them together. His dad was taking a selfie, smiling up at the camera, the wrinkles around his eyes deepening with his big smile. His mum was nuzzled into him, a smile on her face too, staring at him with what was obviously love. He froze, staring at the picture. Did they still love each other?

Jodie's movement brought him away from his family. She was busy arranging photo frames amongst books and strange trinkets on the new shelving units she had installed. He had the sudden urge to sit with her and show her all these pictures. To talk about their childhoods and what they wanted from their future. "Do you want anything to eat?" he whispered to her, breaking their silence.

She shook her head, continuing to arrange books on his shelves. "No, I'll be done in a minute and out of your hair. I said I would cover a shift tonight at the pub. Thanks though."

"Jodie, I can make some lunch," he said softly, not wanting her to leave.

"I'm fine, thank you."

"If you're sure." He didn't press further.

A short while later she whispered to him, "It's finished. Except that blanket would normally be over the back of the chair." She pointed to the blanket Max was under, still sleeping. "But I thought it best to keep it on him."

Tony set his laptop to one side and got up to look around properly. He walked around the room, touching little objects, running his hand along the rough wood, looking at the pictures she had reframed.

Every inch of it felt right. Every inch of it felt like Jodie. And he would have to stay here forever seeing her in every single detail, torturing himself with the memories of how he had messed up. Because he had. He'd ruined whatever they had and whatever they could have had. All for what? Some misguided perception that happiness didn't come from being with someone forever.

His bare feet melted into the new rug she had placed in front of the fire, and he felt the familiar tugging in his trousers. He would never be able to see that rug without imagining Jodie sprawled on it. Naked. Waiting.

"It's amazing, Jodie," he told her, coming to lean on the bannister next to where she was standing.

"Does it feel like home?" she asked, looking up at him through those long lashes of hers.

"At the moment…yes," he whispered, staring intently back at her.

"I'm glad. You two deserve a home to feel comfortable and happy in." She broke her gaze and began gathering the last of her bits from the room and placed them at the front door. "I'll be back again tomorrow, if that's okay, to make a start on the bedroom."

He stayed where he was, still leaning on the bannister, his hands in his pockets. "Of course. We'll look forward to it."

Jodie bent down over Max, placing a small, soft kiss on his head. Then she looked up at Tony, obviously unsure how to say goodbye to him. She raised her hand in the air and gave it an awkward little wave. "Bye then."

She opened the door and let herself out. Tony watched her leave, the house feeling less like home every step she walked away.

CHAPTER 31

Jodie stood outside Tony's house the next morning, praying that today would be less awkward. She was mentally exhausted from yesterday. Exhausted from walking on eggshells the whole day, making sure she didn't disturb Max and end up upsetting Tony. And exhausted from the day she found Max—her arms still hurt from the strain of carrying him. Knocking on the door quietly, she held her breath, not sure what to expect.

Tony welcomed her with a warm smile, and Max stood on his new chair, his tail wagging, anticipating a stroke. What a difference a day could make. Tony was in better spirits this morning—the bags under his eyes weren't as dark and his hair wasn't as ruffled as yesterday. Max looked a bit better too, although he was still hobbling around.

Not having the energy to be around them too much, Jodie shut herself away in Tony's bedroom, sighing as she looked around at the tidy space. Back to the white work. She taped up the floor and heaved the bed frame from the wall, covering it with a sheet—her muscles smarted from carrying Max. Then she sat down on the floor, finally able to make a start on painting. As she did so, the door opened and Tony and Max came in with a steaming cup of coffee and a bacon sandwich for her. She accepted them with thanks as Tony looked around.

"You're a speedy worker," he remarked. "Sorry that took me so long to bring up, I had to lift Max up the stairs and then run down to grab it." He sat on the bed looking at her as she ate.

"You didn't have to."

"I know, but I knew you wouldn't have eaten already." He shrugged it off.

She chewed on some bacon. "I think I'll be able to get a lot of the painting done today," she told him. "Seeing as it's a lot smaller than the living room, and I don't have to do as much detailing." Their conversations had become awkward. She didn't know what to say to him. Something hung in the air between them, needing to be addressed. Would they ever be like they were before?

"Jodie?" Tony pulled her out of her thoughts. "I need to apologise."

Suddenly losing her appetite, she put the last of her sandwich down. She didn't want to do this right now. Her palms grew clammy. Standing up, she brushed him off. "It's fine, Tony, I get it, really. There's nothing to apologise for." She turned her back on him, desperately wishing for him to get the hint and leave her be. There was plenty to apologise for, she knew that. She just didn't have the strength to go through it now.

"Yes there is," he told her. "I've treated you horribly and I'm so sorry. It's not acceptable."

She kept her back to him, pretending she was going to start painting.

"Please can we talk about this?" He spun her around and placed her on the bed next to him, pinning her down with his stare.

"I don't have the strength for this, Tony. Please just leave it. I understand it all, okay? So just drop it."

He didn't give up. "I'm sorry for the way I behaved. A man should never shout at a woman like that." He shook his head, obviously disappointed in himself. "I've never felt such pain and worry as that day, and I took it all out on you. You didn't deserve that. I know you didn't lose Max on purpose. I know you would do anything to protect him. I..." He paused, taking a deep breath before continuing. "I took it out on the person I was closest to and cared the most about. That's not acceptable. I can see how much I've hurt you, and I'll continually try to work to make up for that."

"Tony," she moaned, just wanting him to stop. She should be gushing at his words, she should be feeling little butterflies at him admitting he cared for her. But she couldn't. She wasn't able to process this. Not right now. She wasn't sure why, but she just wanted him to stop talking and let her paint. "Please stop, I can't do this." Tears spilled from her eyes and rolled down her cheeks. She didn't even know why she was crying. All she felt was confusion...and exhaustion.

He swept the tears away with the pad of his thumb, cupping her cheek. The warmth of his rough hand passed through her, his scent filling her senses. She could easily have wrapped herself around him, absorbing all the comfort he offered.

"What's going on?" he asked quietly, concern in his eyes.

"I don't know," she answered honestly.

"You're shutting me out." His hand hadn't left her cheek.

She could have laughed at him. He had shut her out first. "I just don't know what's going on," she told him. "I'm exhausted from the back and forth, the fighting, the day Max ran off, with work, with juggling everything, with not knowing where I stand with you. My heart keeps telling me you like me and my head tells me you don't. That I'm being used and I need to protect myself. And I'm not sure that will ever fade away. I agreed to that one night, but I don't think I should have. I thought I would be okay, but I'm not. I'm hurt and sad and lonely. I can't think anymore. I can't feel anymore...all I want to do is paint." Tears rolled freely as she tried to verbalise her thoughts, knowing that her words were as messy when she spoke them as they had been in her head.

"Oh, Jodie," he replied, scooping her towards him more. "I never wanted to hurt you. I hope you believe me when I say that." He stared deep into her eyes. "I understand you need time to process all this, and I'll give you that. Just please know I'm here and I'll do whatever I can to make you feel better. I'm sorry." He wrapped her in a comforting embrace, warming her heart. It had felt like an eternity since he touched her, and her skin yearned for him.

She pulled away from him. "I've heard everything you've said," she told him. "Just give me some time to process?" she asked again.

Nodding, he got up from the bed. When he got to the door, he turned back, looking at her as she got ready to paint. He looked like he wanted to say something further, but was struggling to decide whether he should or not.

"What?" she said. "It's best just to get it all out now, so we don't have to do this again."

"I…" he croaked, then shook his head. "I should never have asked for one night." Her heart took a nosedive once again. "Because I never wanted just one." He ushered Max out without further comment and closed the door behind them.

She stood for a minute. She was pretty sure this was Tony baring his soul to her, opening himself up and letting her in.

She started to paint, knowing if she didn't start now, she wouldn't finish.

So, he had always wanted more from her. Why couldn't he have said that from the get-go? He was so complex, he seemed to want to close himself off to everyone apart from Max so that he didn't have a meaningful connection with anyone. And yet they were developing one anyway. Weren't they?

It felt like they had been, but she could never tell if it was her heart trying to trick her. This was what she'd wanted from the start. She would have thrown herself at him ages ago, if she had the confidence he liked her. But now? Now he had finally opened up, she was weary and jaded. Already she had been hurt. Could she really put herself up for something worse?

She sighed, hating how whiney she had become. But when she was with him, she felt she could achieve anything, that she was strong and brave and beautiful. She laughed with him and Max. They felt like home. God, she was confused.

She continued painting for what felt like hours, her mind busy with back and forth, her hands carrying on without command.

When she finished the white work, she sat on the bed, staring dumbfounded at the wall she needed to paint next. It would be a mid-grey colour, to draw the room in and make it feel cosy.

The door opened and Tony came in again carrying a tray of biscuits and drinks, Max hobbling behind him.

"Have you even moved?" he joked.

"I've done all the detailing," she retorted.

"I'm joking." He placed the tray on his bedside table. "I can smell the paint."

She needed to get used to his sense of humour again, their banter. How could it feel like so much time had passed, when in reality it had just been a few days?

"Sit and have a snack with us before you start on the walls," he said, pulling off the cover on the bed so they could sit comfortably. "Max has been crying at the bottom of the stairs since I took him back down. He misses you." He placed a tray with coffee and biscuits on one of the new bedside tables she'd had delivered, and then lifted Max up on the bed with them so that he could snuggle next to Jodie. Max instantly fell asleep, with her stroking his ears. "Lucky bugger," he mumbled, looking at Max lying on her thigh.

Jodie smiled, trying to think of some witty comeback to respond with…but nothing came to her.

"How are you feeling?" Tony asked, shuffling his position so he could look at her.

"Thoroughly brain dead."

"You don't have to be here, you know? I won't be offended if you want to go home and finish up early. It's just paint."

She met his eyes. He meant it. But his eyes also told her that he didn't actually want her to leave.

"I want to be here," she admitted.

"Good! We want you here."

She loved how he spoke on Max's behalf. She nibbled at a biscuit, trying to keep her hands busy. Not knowing what else to say, she said, "The man will be here tomorrow to expose the brick work." She had booked in a builder to do that task. Knowing her luck, she'd chip at a bit of plaster and cause the wall to collapse. He was going to expose the brick behind the bed, to make a feature wall. The more rustic and messy, the better. Jodie would then come back and paint her second coat. Furniture would be delivered shortly after and she could come back and do her last bits of staging.

"Yes," he sighed. "I remembered that." He waited a moment. "Is this what we've been reduced to? Talking about work?" He had a pained expression on his face.

"We'll get there," she promised. "We just have to figure out our relationship."

"How do you mean?"

"We started off as friends, then I became your employee, and then you became my first client, then I was your dog sitter and then we fought, and then we…you know."

"Had sex?" He raised his eyebrow.

She gulped. "Yep. And then you hated me and now we're…" She shrugged, her sentence hanging in the air.

"I never hated you," he said. She rolled her eyes at him. "I didn't, I just needed someone to blame." He pulled her towards him, making her lean on his shoulder, wrapping his arm around her and resting his hand on her hip. Max woke up with a huff and went to lay in a patch of sun streaming through the window.

They sat there for a while, listening to the bird song filtering through the window and the sound of Max now snoring.

"What was your favourite relationship?" he asked quietly, beginning to trace his fingers over her slightly exposed hip where her t-shirt had risen. She blushed into his chest, thankful he couldn't see her face.

"I can see you blushing, remember?" His voice was soft and husky.

She stayed still. "I'm not blushing," she told him, knowing full well that she was.

"I have a cracking view from here."

Looking down, she noticed her reddening boobs trying to get free from her v-neck shirt. She swatted at his chest while adjusting her top to a more appropriate position.

"I'm sorry," he laughed, trying to shield himself. "I couldn't help myself."

"What, from being a pervert?"

"Well, that, and making you blush more."

She shuffled further back on the bed, but he pulled her back by the hand.

"Hey, you're not going anywhere. I like having you in my bed."

She laid back on his shoulder. "It's not going to be that easy."

"I know." He was tracing her hip again. "I wouldn't say any of this has been easy though…would you?"

She shook her head, enjoying the feeling of connecting with him again.

"It feels right though," he whispered into her hair, sending shivers down her spine.

They sat like that for a while, Tony tracing lazy circles over her hip, Jodie listening to the thudding of his heart. Max had taken himself to the landing, settling himself in his dog bed that Jodie had placed there so it didn't get ruined. She should be painting, but she couldn't resist just being here with him.

"Jodie?"

"Yeah?" she murmured sleepily. The warm breeze blew in gently through the open window, birds chirping outside.

"I know you don't think I open up to you, or that you know anything about me really. But…" He paused. "You're the closest I've ever been with someone. Well…a woman. Ever."

She twisted herself around to look up at him. They were so close their breaths entwined around each other. "Am I?" She desperately wanted it to be true.

He nodded, stroking a strand of hair away from her face. "I never thought I would end up with someone." He stared intently at the strand in his fingers, not meeting her eyes. "I didn't think there was any space in my life. It was just me and Max against the world, and he was my support through the hard times and my buddy through the good. I never thought I needed someone else."

She let him talk, not wanting to disturb his train of

thought and the words he obviously needed to say. As he spoke her heart filled with love for him.

"I always thought relationships were more hassle than they were worth. I had quite a privileged lifestyle growing up. I went to grammar school and university, I never needed for anything and money was never an issue. But my mum and dad never really seemed happy in each other's company, even though lots of people would have traded places for their lifestyle, thinking it could only bring about happiness. I always got the impression they were together for me, and then when I was old enough for them to split up without it impacting on me too much, they still just stayed together for convenience." He sighed. "I never wanted that, but it just seemed inevitable."

"All relationships are different, Tony," she replied. "You never know what's going on behind closed doors. Maybe your mum and dad are happy in some way, it just might not present itself in the way you think it should, or maybe it's private between them. To be married for so long, they must get along at some point or other."

He played with her hair. "My mum emailed me some photos yesterday, ones I hadn't seen before of me as a baby, and they looked so happy. Even my dad looked content. There was this one picture of me on a blanket and they sat off in the distance, snuggling together. I had never seen them look at each other like that. It was obvious they loved each other. So I looked at the pictures of them on their recent holiday. I found one of the both of them, looking so happy and in love. So maybe you're right. Maybe I don't know what goes on behind closed doors."

Unable to resist, she stroked his rough cheek where his stubble was growing back. It made him look raw and rough but handsome as hell. "You realise you've spent a long time avoiding getting into a relationship where you would feel lonely…by just being lonely?" She gave a little laugh.

Turning his body, he scooted down the bed so that they were facing each other and held her close. "Yeah, I suppose I have."

"And you realise," she breathed, mesmerised by the feel of his body pressed against hers, "that I have tried to get you to open up to me for so long…and the one time I want you to not talk, you then tell me everything…without me even having to ask?"

He laughed with her. And then stopped, staring into her eyes. Her body warmed all over and she bit her lip. "You're paying me to be painting, you know."

He thumbed her lip, stopping her from biting it. "Painting can wait. I'm enjoying having you in my bed too much."

"This is getting dangerous." She was desperate to kiss him again. All she had to do was inch forward slightly and she could meet his lips and taste him.

"I know." His voice was gravelly. He cupped the back of her neck, sending goosebumps all over her body. "I can't help myself." Neither of them moved.

She needed to break this up, but her body wouldn't let her. "Tony," she pleaded, hoping maybe he had the self-control to stop. "How do I know it won't just be one more night?" As much as she wanted to reach out and kiss him and spend the whole day and night with him again, she couldn't let herself face any more heartache. Not at the moment.

He rolled her over so she was lying on her back and his body was half pressed against hers, the bulge in his trousers prodding her hip. He searched her eyes. "It was never going to be just one night, and it was never going to be just one more night. I need every night with you, Jodie. You have invaded every part of my life and you can't leave."

She kissed him then, unable to resist him any longer,

letting her tongue explore his mouth, pulling little groans from him as he lost himself in her too. She broke away from him, her hands either side of his face. His eyes were full of joy, like the cat that got the cream. "You make me sound like an alien, invading your life," she laughed.

"A hot, sexy alien." And he pounced on her, devouring her once more.

CHAPTER 32

Tony stirred from his nap when Jodie snuggled in closer to him. He lifted his arm and pulled her closer. "Mmmm, I love the way you feel lying on me," he murmured, his voice groggy from sleep. She wrapped her leg over his thighs and stroked his toned tummy. "When's that chimney sweep coming?" he asked her lazily, brushing his fingers over her body, memorising every inch of her.

"I haven't contacted any yet. I'll probably do that in the next couple of months." She nudged him to behave.

"Do I really have to wait that long?" he asked, nibbling at her neck.

She elbowed him again. "We're coming up to summer. You can't possibly want to put the fire on!"

"Oh I really, really do." He twisted her around, kissing her hard.

They couldn't resist each other, like the world depended on them always touching or being close to be able to survive. Making up for all the time they wouldn't allow themselves to indulge in each other.

He eventually let her go, so she could have her long-awaited shower while he made them lunch.

As the water ran and trickled down the pipes in the kitchen wall, he had to resist the urge to go back up and jump in there with her. He liked having Jodie in his home—something felt different and comforting. *Home.* He'd never thought of it as a home before, it was always just his house. Yet when she was here, with him and Max, it felt like home. Safe and sound, a place of contentment. A place he didn't want to leave. He was sure it wasn't just because she had decorated the living room. It was *her* that made it home.

He had been so stupid to try and hide his feelings for her, to treat her like she didn't matter, like he hadn't fallen for her. He could have lost her, and now he had to make sure she knew how he felt so he didn't lose her. Ever.

When he finished making lunch, he went back upstairs and found her sitting on his bed. She sat staring at the wall, obviously lost in her thoughts, blow drying her hair. Her stunning body was hidden in his large navy towel. He would never tire of looking at her, drinking in her beauty.

Silently, he wrapped his arms around her body, startling her. Batting him away, she tried to carry on drying her hair, but she was too irresistible to him. He came back to nibble at her bare shoulders and neck.

"Food's almost ready," he whispered, trailing kisses up her neck, little bumps appearing wherever he kissed. Twinges of need grew in him down below as she continued focusing on her task, almost like a challenge to him.

"That was quick."

"You were in the shower for ages." He started sucking at her ear lobe, taking advantage of the fact she was drying the other side of her hair.

"I couldn't help it, the water felt too good." Her breath

quickened at his attention, her chest rising and falling while she tried to keep focused.

"Hmm," he murmured against her, the image of her covered in droplets of water, soap running down her naked body, vivid in his mind. He should have ditched the food and devoured her like he'd wanted. "I bet it did," he growled, biting at her neck.

She yelped in surprise. "I'm not the food, by the way," she laughed, rubbing at the spot he'd bitten.

He pulled her sharply down the bed so she was lying across it, her legs hanging off. Pouncing on top of her, he tore the towel open to reveal her naked body underneath. "Oh yes you are." Bending down over her body, he sucked and nipped and kissed all along her.

"Tony," she moaned, trying to wiggle away from his attention. "What about the food?"

"Let me love you," he whispered across her skin in response.

"Okay." She didn't hesitate. She needed him as much as he needed her.

He edged further down towards her hot, slick centre, every touch sending her body jumping.

"Tony," she urged him.

He laughed at her obvious desire. "Patience," he commanded. His pace grew slower as he inched ever closer to her. He enjoyed tormenting her, building her need till she begged him.

"Please?" she whimpered when he was finally hovering over her opening.

He opened her legs further, exposing her fully to him.

She smiled, obviously thinking she had won and he had given in.

Not that easily, my love. "What do you want me to do?" he whispered across her sensitive flesh, loving the look of desire lighting her emerald eyes. He stared deep into her soul. When the only response he got was her embarrassed blush, he blew over her folds. The softness of the air made her shudder with need.

She took a steadying breath, then looked him dead in the eye. "Make me come!"

A wicked smile crept across his face. "You never disappoint," he told her, before finally giving her what she needed.

As he swiped his tongue from her opening up to her clitoris, tasting all of her, her body juddered. He licked her again, but this time as his tongue pushed past her entrance he slid his fingers deep inside of her, massaging and pulsing as he circled her with his tongue. Her moans grew louder as he stepped up his pace. She was close. He built her up, devouring her in the most intimate way possible.

"Tony!" she cried. "I'm going to come."

He didn't relent, pushing her over the edge where her body shattered in pleasure, bucking against him. He eased his pace slightly, so she didn't miss a single moment of orgasm.

His tongue softened as he watched her recover, her skin slightly pink from her pleasure, her nipples budded. As she came back to reality, he stopped his lapping and withdrew his fingers. He crawled up her body and kissed her. "You're incredible," he whispered in her ear. She lay stretched out beneath him, her eyes closed, a peaceful smile on her red lips.

"No, *you* are," she said, as she patted him on the back lazily in jest. "Good job."

He laughed into her neck and then looked up into her eyes adoringly. "I'm falling for you, Jodie," he told her, not breaking eye contact. He had to tell her how he felt. "I know it's fast...I know it's unexpected, but it's true. Scary...but true."

Her eyes filled with tears, searching his, questioning if it really was true. He had hurt her so much that he didn't expect her to say anything back. She needed time to trust him, trust his words, his feelings for her. And he would give her that time. He would give her anything.

Silently, she placed her hands either side of his face and pulled him down to her, kissing him lovingly. Her kiss said a thousand words. She felt the same too.

When they broke apart, she rested her forehead against his and pressed her hand to his heart. It pounded fiercely against her palm. She took a deep breath. "I feel the same," she whispered.

Sighing in relief, he collapsed in a heap on top of her, his body crushing hers.

"Tony!" She flailed about, trying to get him off.

"Thank God for that." He looked down at her, grinning as he eased his body weight. She didn't have to say it, but boy did it feel good that she had. "Let's eat." He pulled her up from the bed, still naked, and pressed her against his fully clothed body.

"I would have thought you were full up." She snuggled into his neck as they hugged, and he rubbed her back and bum, needing to feel every part of her.

His laugh rumbled through his chest. "I'm always ravenous."

Tony had made them chicken and potatoes with green beans and a creamy spinach sauce. It looked and tasted divine and they ate it up greedily, with a bottle of red wine.

"So what happens tomorrow?" Jodie frowned, pushing the last few green beans around in the creamy, garlicky sauce. As happy as she felt, nagging doubt kept sounding in her head. She had felt this happy before, but then disaster had struck.

"With what?" He had already finished his whole plate and had seconds.

"Us?" she murmured, still not meeting his eyes.

He held her hand across the table so that she had to stop playing with her food. "You're worried something is going to happen to ruin this?"

He was always able to tell exactly what she was thinking, but right now she was grateful that she didn't have to find the words. She nodded.

"I can't promise that won't happen," he told her gently, stroking the back of her hand with his thumb. "But I can promise that I will fight for us, and do everything in my power to keep us strong and happy. Relationships will always have ups and downs, but I'm along for the ride if you are?"

She would have loved to have heard promises of it all being okay, of them living happily ever after. But this was real, and he would have been lying if he promised that. It would take them time to settle and heal from the past few days, but she knew they could, and she knew that they had healed a great deal already.

"I'm along for the ride too," she told him, squeezing his hand before letting it go to devour her last remnants of food.

CHAPTER 33

The next morning, Jodie and Tony awoke naked in each other's arms, twisted together, clutching on for dear life. They were sleepy from the night before, staying up late, learning new things about each other. Jodie had pushed him down underneath her, and teased and pleasured him the way he had her just a few hours before.

"What's the plan today?"

"Well." She sighed, knowing it was going to be a busy one and although they both would have preferred it, they couldn't just spend all day in bed. "We have the builder coming over to do your wall, I have my shower being fitted, I need to try and get back on track with your painting, and I have to prepare for my mum and dad coming over tomorrow for lunch."

Kissing her gently, Tony calmed her panic. "Well," he told her when they broke apart, "you can't do any painting while the builder is here. You'll get in his way. So you might as well go and get your shower sorted and everything planned for tomorrow. I'll stay here for the guy in case he needs anything. Why don't you think about getting someone in to finish the painting here?"

"I want to finish the project myself," she insisted. "I've done all this hard work and then you don't want me to finish it?"

"It's not that I don't want you to finish it," he replied gently. "I just know what you're like and you normally spread yourself too thin. You have that important meeting to prepare for as well, and you have a lot going on at home. Besides, whenever you're in my bedroom, I end up devouring you and you don't get anything done anyway." He nibbled her ear promisingly.

"Maybe that's why I want to be here," she told him, blushing under his gaze.

"You're playing with fire." His eyes smouldered.

"I like it hot," she retorted and he kissed her passionately, his arousal evident on her hip.

Then he pulled away from her with a groan. "Why don't I sort out the builder today, and we can always paint another day? Then when you're free you can come and join me. Hopefully by that time the builder will be gone and all we'll have on our to-do list is do each other." He raised his eyebrows cheekily.

Jodie busied herself tidying her cottage so that she could return to Tony's as soon as Mark was finished with installing her shower. She already missed him so much. Everything she did or touched, her mind went back to him. Was he as distracted as she was?

Her phone vibrated in her pocket. A call from her mum. "I was just checking in on you and to see if you're still up for tomorrow. I haven't heard from you."

"I know. Sorry Mum, I've been so busy." She leant against her kitchen cabinets, Mark's banging and clashing sounding above her.

"What's that noise?" Sandra asked, and Jodie explained what Mark was doing. "That will be nice then," her mum said. "Your first shower will feel like heaven."

"I already had one yesterday," she replied without thinking.

"Oh, really? Where?"

Shit. Her mum was always on the lookout for a bit of gossip. "I had one at Tony's." It was no use lying—she never could lie to her mother.

"Oh." She didn't sound too surprised. Perhaps she'd thought that Jodie's silence meant they had made up and she wasn't in dire straits anymore. "You two sorted it out then?"

"Yes, we made up." She'd have to tell her mum about her and Tony at some point. But maybe not right now.

"And how's the sex?"

"Mum!" Jodie shouted down the phone, shocked by the blunt question.

"Well, really," she replied. "I'm not a fool. It's obvious you had feelings for him. And how could he not like you back?" Sandra scoffed. "You are sleeping together, aren't you?"

"If you must know, then yes," she replied, mortified.

"Good!" her mum said, shocking her again.

"Mother!"

"I'm not a prude, you know. I've had my fair share of men, thank you!"

"Oh my God," Jodie muttered, willing the world to swallow her up.

"I'm just glad you're letting someone in at last," Sandra told her. "You're a bit closed off to the opposite sex, you know."

Jodie hadn't thought about it before, but maybe her mum was right. She and Tony were quite similar in that respect.

"Is he coming over tomorrow? We'd like to meet him."

"I hadn't thought about it, to be honest." Was it too early for Tony to be meeting her parents? It might scare him off. She chewed her lip.

"Well, we want to meet him, and Max too. We'll bring lunch with us, and will aim to get to you for twelve, okay?" That was her mum's way of telling her Tony had better be there.

"Okay, Mum."

They said their goodbyes, then Jodie timidly typed a text to Tony.

So my mum and dad want to meet you tomorrow.

She waited for a reply, staring out past her garden at the swooping birds in the field behind her house. The ding of her mobile took her out of her daydream.

And what do you want?

She typed a quick reply. *I want you to do what you want to do.*

She hadn't even put her phone in her back pocket when it dinged again. *I take that as a 'you want me to come'. And I want to meet them too.*

Her heart filled with joy. She had never let a boy meet her parents before. Man. He was definitely all man. She got another text. *I miss you already.*

She replied. *I miss you too.* Then she went around the house, finishing her tasks practically walking on air.

Tony sat on his bed, watching Jodie in amusement as she rushed around like a mad woman, getting ready to see her mum and dad.

"Calm down," he told her. "It's all going to be fine."

She wouldn't listen though. She was too busy brushing Max's fur to get him looking as adorable as possible. Just like a worried mum who wanted her child to be on their best behaviour. His heart melted.

"You don't know what they're like," she told him, still busy grooming Max, who was enjoying the attention but every time moved it would dislodge his perfectly styled hair.

"From what you've told me, they're fine and relaxed and there is nothing to worry about." He tried to placate her again, but she was having none of it.

"Well, yes." She looked round at him. "But I don't know what they'll be like with you." She pointed the dog brush at him. "I've never brought anyone home for them to meet. They might be a nightmare." She went back to brushing Max, carefully skirting over his still-plastered leg.

Tony laughed, which earned him a threatening stare. "You're worrying for worrying's sake." He scooted over to her and pulled the brush from her hand. As soon as she stopped brushing Max, he shook his whole body and his fur puffed out, making him resemble a big ball of brown cotton candy. Jodie sighed.

"Have you ever met anyone's parents before?" she asked, not meeting his eyes.

"No." He shook his head and kissed her flushed cheek. "I don't date, remember?"

She laughed. "How are you so calm?" She let him nuzzle into her neck.

"I have faith in us, and I know your parents will see that."

A short while later, they walked the short distance to Jodie's cottage, Tony carrying Max. All of her hard work had been ruined—Max looked just as scruffy as he normally did. Jodie was still nervous, he could feel it radiating from her and could see it when he looked her in the eye. She never had been able to hide anything from him.

Nothing he had done made any difference. He had even pounced on her and made her forget the whole world existed for a few minutes, but as soon as she had screamed out his name and he felt the ripples of her orgasm subsiding, she was back to worrying again.

She let them into her silent cottage and did a quick once-around, trying to make sure nothing was out of place. Tony knew it was best to leave her to it rather than attempting to get her to stop, so he and Max sat on the sofa, watching her.

Eventually the knock came at the door, and Jodie froze mid-plumping a cushion, her eyes big and round.

"It will be fine, I promise," Tony whispered before she opened the door.

CHAPTER 34

Her parents were finally here. She didn't think her heart could take it anymore. She had never been so nervous in her life. Like her whole future depended on this moment. Like her life would be ruined if her parents hated Tony.

Which was silly, she knew. They would adore Tony. Wouldn't they?

Hugging them and welcoming them in, she stood to one side to introduce them to Tony. Max was standing on the sofa next to him, whimpering with excitement, while Tony held him back so he didn't jump off and hurt his leg.

"Mum, Dad, this is Tony and Max. Tony, this is my mum Sandra and my dad Robert."

"Nice to meet you." Tony kissed Sandra on the cheek and shook Robert's hand. They both bent down to greet Max too and coo over his bandaged leg.

"Sorry," Tony said. "I'm trying to keep him calm so he doesn't hurt himself."

"Don't worry, lad," Robert said happily. "We're dog lovers, aren't we Sandra?"

Sandra had sat down next to Max to enable him to sniff her and to give him love and attention. Tony let his collar go and sat down while Robert took a seat on the other sofa.

"Drinks?" Jodie asked and went out to make cups of tea for everyone and get lunch sorted. She strained to listen to their conversation but the boiling kettle drowned their voices out. They were laughing; that was a good sign. She released the breath she was holding.

Her mum and dad had brought cheese and crackers, olives and a meat selection. She laid it out on plates and took it all into the living room to place on the coffee table.

"It's lovely in here, Jodie," her dad told her. "You need to give me a tour."

"Oh, yes," she replied, flustered.

"Give her a minute, Robert," Sandra told him, motioning for Jodie to take a seat next to Tony. "Have a tour after lunch."

"Of course." Robert sat back.

They all helped themselves and Tony lifted Max onto the floor while they ate. He stared wistfully at the meat platter, wagging his tail.

"Tony was telling us about the amazing work you're doing at his house." Sandra filled Jodie in. "He says you've totally transformed the space already, and it feels more and more like home every day."

Jodie blushed at his sentiment. "That's very kind of him." She spread some cheese onto a cracker. "I thought he would have told you all about The Dog."

"What, the pub?" Her dad's ears pricked up.

"Yes," Jodie replied. "Tony owns it."

"Does he?" Her dad seemed genuinely surprised.

"Yes. Did Mum not tell you?"

"No." Her dad shook his head at the same time as Sandra said, "Yes I did!"

Her parents were often like this—they had been together for a long time and had settled into their marriage. They loved each other dearly, that much was obvious, but Sandra often complained that Robert didn't listen to her and Robert often complained that Sandra talked too much.

"Well Dad, Tony owns the pub over the road. We can go there for a drink later on, can't we Tony?"

"Of course. I'll text John to save us a table. It gets busy on a Saturday afternoon."

"You don't have to do that," Robert said, but the look on his face betrayed the fact that he was very keen to go and visit.

"It's not a problem, really," Tony reassured him and quickly typed a text before putting his phone away.

They talked some more as they ate, catching up, her parents learning more about Tony and how he and Jodie had met. The more they talked, the less on edge she felt, finally relaxing into her seat now that everyone seemed to be getting on.

Once they had all finished eating, Jodie took her dad around her little cottage, giving him the tour of her new home. He was very happy for her, and just like her mum and Kelsie had done a few days before, he complimented and praised in all the right places. Sitting back down, Jodie felt content, a big smile on her face.

"Can I give Max a little treat?" Sandra asked Tony. Max's ears perked up at the word. Jodie noticed that she had left a little pile of Italian meat on her plate, obviously on purpose.

"Of course," Tony replied. Max understood he was allowed and walked over to Sandra, wagging his tail.

"Are you sure, Tony?" Jodie asked. She wasn't sure if Italian ham would be the best thing for him to eat.

"Surely I can give him a little treat?" Sandra said to her, almost batting her eyelashes to try and get her way. "He's been through so much recently. Anyway, he is practically my grandson, I'm allowed to spoil him." She turned for confirmation to Tony, who nodded with a smile, unfazed.

"Mum!" Jodie shook her head, embarrassed at her mother's choice of words. "He's a dog, not a grandson."

"Well, when you think about it," Tony said in her mother's defence, "he is like our child." Jodie was taken aback. Tony turned back to her mum. "You should have seen the way she was preening him this morning so he looked his best to meet you two." They all chuckled at her.

"I was not!" she said haughtily.

"You were. I'm the doting father and you're his nurturing mother. He comes to you for comfort all the time." Max had finished eating his treat and now moved closer to Jodie, leaning his head on her thigh for a stroke. "See?" Tony laughed, knowing Max had proved his point. "We'd be lost without you."

Her heart melted at their show of affection for her. Giving into Max, she stroked his soft ears and smiled at Tony. Out of the corner of her eye she could see her mum smiling at them too. Her dad had gone back for seconds, and continued eating, completely and wonderfully oblivious.

"Shall we go to the pub then?" Tony asked.

Her dad's ears pricked up, like Max's had done at the word 'treat'. "Oh yes," he replied, setting his plate down.

Jodie and her mum quickly tidied the plates away and they all walked to the pub for a drink, Tony once again carrying Max. It would be Max's first time back at the pub so everyone would want to see him and see how he was recovering. Jodie was also acutely aware that this would be the first 'outing' they'd have as a couple. She wasn't even sure what to refer to their relationship as. Were they just seeing each other, or were they keeping it secret?

She bit her lip the closer to the pub they got, her anxiety increasing with every step. Her parents were blissfully unaware, but Tony seemed to sense her worry and dropped his pace to fall in line with her.

"It will be fine," he promised, not even breaking a sweat carrying Max. She looked up at him, and his deep eyes reassured her slightly. "I don't want to keep this a secret," he added. "But if you want to then I will."

CHAPTER 35

Jodie looked up at him, stunning in the spring sunshine, hope in her eyes. "What is *this?*" she barely whispered.

"It's obvious, isn't it?"

She shook her head, blushing, his favourite thing she did.

He smiled down at her. His heart belonged to this wonderful, sexy, talented woman in front of him. "I love you, Jodie. I think I loved you the moment I saw you. We both did."

Max looked up at them both. Thank God Max had had the good sense to bring them together.

Jodie kissed him. "I love you too."

Max whimpered in his arms, jealous.

"And you, Max." She kissed the top of his tufty head.

When they reached the pub, Jodie opened the door for them all. Once inside, Tony placed Max gently on the floor.

"Calm, Max," Tony told him, trying to avoid him getting overly excited. Then he showed Sandra and Robert over to the bar. "John," Tony called him over. "This is Jodie's mum and dad, Sandra and Robert. This is John, he's the manager around here. Have whatever you like, it's on the house." Robert patted his back in appreciation. "I'm just going to do the rounds, if that's okay? I haven't been in for a while." He left them ordering with John and went to greet some of the regulars.

After a short while and managing to keep the small talk to a minimum, he returned to John to order a drink. Sophie was in her usual spot sitting at the bar so she could spend some time with her brother. Max had settled himself in the corner of the pub with Jodie and her parents, his head on her shoe.

"How's he doing?" Sophie asked as John pulled the pint.

"Better now he's resting properly." It was like he had needed to see Jodie to be able to rest when he got back from the vet's, and as soon as she came round to decorate he'd improved so much.

Taking the pint from John, Tony saw the familiar little smirk on his face. But for some reason it didn't send him crazy as it did before.

"You two look happy," John said.

"Yeah." He couldn't hold back his smile.

John nodded his head knowingly. "I'm glad you let her in, mate. She's perfect for you."

Looking back again at Jodie, who was happy and relaxed with her parents, Tony had to admit she was pretty perfect. "You're getting a bit soppy, John."

"How come I don't get this level of support with Scott?" Sophie scoffed.

Tony ruffled her hair playfully. "Because Scott doesn't deserve you. And when you find the guy you're actually meant to be with, John and I will be supportive, we promise. Won't we, John?"

"We promise."

Tony laughed, tapped the bar and left them.

∾

Jodie's dad was sulking that they had to leave. They'd had a lovely couple of hours sitting in the pub, laughing and getting to know each other. She and Tony walked her parents to their car, with promises that they could return whenever they wanted to. Tony had already dropped Max home so he could rest properly on his new favourite armchair.

Jodie's mum gave her a tight hug when they reached the car, and whispered, "I'm really proud of you, never forget that. This place is beautiful and it all just feels right. This is fate, my darling daughter, I am sure of it." She gave her one last squeeze before releasing her to give Tony a kiss. It warmed Jodie to think her mum approved. She knew it shouldn't matter, but it was still nice to know.

They waved her parents off, Tony's arm wrapped around her lower back holding her hip as a cold wind rippled over them. The sun was sitting lower in the sky now and wasn't as warm as earlier in the day. Tony pulled her close to share his warmth.

"Why don't you stay at mine again?" he murmured into her ear.

"I need to get prepared for this meeting I have on Tuesday." She had stayed a few nights at his place and didn't want to intrude too much.

"Max and I won't disturb you. We can stay at yours if you prefer?" There was a longing in his voice. Not sexual, just a longing to be together.

"No, I'll come to yours," she replied. "Max will be happier there, and he needs his rest after today."

She went back home and packed another overnight bag, while Tony went back to his house to check on Max.

As she came back down her stairs, she looked around her newly decorated living room. She was proud of this home, what it symbolised and how it had turned out. Yet without Max and Tony here, it didn't feel quite the same. It felt abandoned and stale. She sighed. Who knew where they would spend most of their time if it all worked out with Tony? She wouldn't blame him if he did want to spend more time at his house. But then what would happen to this place? Shutting the curtains and locking up the house, she pulled her jacket around her against the chilling breeze.

Tony had left the latch on for her, so she was able to walk right inside. Max was sleeping on his armchair and Tony lounged on the sofa. He beamed up at her and came to take her bag. Right now, this very second in Tony's home, she felt comfortable, at ease and like this was where she was meant to be. The complete opposite of what she'd felt in her own home.

"What are you thinking about?" Tony whispered as he wrapped his arms around her from behind. She entwined her fingers into his.

"How different this place feels." She had done a good job here. It fit Tony and Max to a tee and he looked more comfortable here now than he did before.

"That's because you're here." He nuzzled her ear.

"It's not." She smiled back at him.

"Well, it's because all three of us are here together…it feels like home." He kissed her temple and surveyed the room with her. They were swaying gently, rocking back and forth.

"Maybe that is what it is." She sighed happily. She didn't really want to think it, but he was right. Stepping in that door just now had felt more like home than her own cottage. Being with her boys, she felt more at home than ever before. They were comfortable together, happy and relaxed.

"You're worrying about your cottage." He was reading her like a book again. She nodded against him. "You don't have to do anything about it now," he said reassuringly.

"It feels so lonely and lost," she told him. It was like their cottages had traded places. Tony's cottage had become warm and safe, while Jodie's had grown cold and stale. It felt like a betrayal. When she'd bought it, her little home had represented so much—her freedom and her dreams—and she had promised to love it and to treat it well. Had she?

"We can stay there if you like?"

She shook her head. She didn't want to, and that was the issue.

"Look." Tony twisted her around so she was facing him. "I won't ever force you to do something you don't want to do. If you ever want to stay there, with me and Max, or just on your own...you can. If in the future you want us to live there together...we will. If you want to live here...we will. You can sell it if you like, or not. Maybe we can run a holiday home." His eyes twinkled with endless possibilities. His openness and laid-back nature made Jodie smile. "But for now," he told her, "you don't have to worry about anything." He kissed her gently. "I promise." He nuzzled her nose, his hands tangled in her hair. "Coffee?"

She nodded and went to sit on the sofa. He put a *Friends* episode on for her and went to make the coffee.

When he returned with their drinks, Jodie turned to him, coffee in hand and asked, "Did you already tell John about us?"

"No, I hadn't said anything to anyone," he replied. She thought as much. He added, "I think he had just sort of read this whole thing between us. Why?" He stroked her hair gently.

"Just something he said in the pub. I just wondered if you had or not." She shrugged it off.

"You asked me not to, remember? And I didn't have the chance to today."

"Well, that was when it was just a one-night stand," she joked.

"Ahh." His eyes grew wide with realisation. "So you now want me to tell people, so everyone knows we're together?"

235

"Well, no," she said, secretly wanting him to tell everyone so it made it official.

He put down his coffee and made a move to stand up. "Shall I go and shout out that Jodie is my girlfriend on the village green?"

"No!" She grabbed him back down. She wouldn't put it past him to actually do it. "Is that what I am?" she asked timidly. They had yet to put a label on their relationship.

"Of course you are!"

"It's just you haven't asked me or said that to me before." Her tummy bubbled with excitement like a little girl.

"I thought it was obvious." He stroked her burning cheek. "Has that been bothering you?" She shrugged. "Jodie?" he whispered, locking his intense gaze to hers. "Will you be my girlfriend?"

"Yes." She beamed. It shouldn't matter, but it did.

He leant down and kissed her passionately. "Now should I go and shout it to everyone?" he asked when they broke apart.

"No!" She nudged him in the ribs, giggling.

EPILOGUE

Tony pulled Jodie in for a hug. "I'm so proud of you," he whispered into her ear. Five months of hard work and she had smashed it. He knew she had been dreading this day, worried that something would go wrong, that something might break or it might not all pull together. But he had had every faith in her, and hopefully now she could have a bit of faith in herself.

They were finally saying goodbye to Louise and the other members of the team that Jodie had worked with on the show homes. They had attended the open event where they'd invited a select few potential buyers, influencers and press to drum up interest in buying the exclusive properties. And throughout the afternoon, all he'd heard was how beautiful everything was, how people wished they could live in a home like this, and even asking if they could buy the home with all the furnishings included.

Just as they were about to walk out the door, Lousie grabbed Jodie again and pulled them to one side. "Sorry to keep you two, but I just wanted to say how much everyone has loved the design, Jodie. We've never had such a successful launch and we're all really excited with how these are going to sell. I think the directors have big plans for you, so don't be surprised if they call you in the next couple of days and ask you to design even more."

Typically, Jodie tried to brush it all off, saying that they must have told that to their previous designer too, but Tony knew they hadn't. What Jodie had done with the properties was outstanding. Each one was unique and had its own flair, and yet he could see Jodie's influences and design choices throughout.

He eventually got her away from the houses and the praise, and took her hand in his as they drove. She gazed dreamily out the window.

"I know you're probably really tired after that," he said, drawing her attention to him, "but John and Sophie wanted to see you and hear about how it all went today. Do you mind popping into the pub for a bit?"

Squeezing his fingers, she said, "Of course not. I'd love that."

An hour later, they pulled up to Winton Green and The Dog and walked hand in hand through the door. Max came bounding up to them, wanting a welcome stroke. They had left him with John at the pub so he didn't get lonely, but it never felt right when he wasn't with them.

Sophie jumped up from the bar stool and came to hug Jodie. "How did it go? Give us all the details." She pulled Jodie to the bar and sat her on a stool, handing her a drink that John had already poured for them.

"She did amazing." Tony kissed the top of Jodie's head and took his pint of beer from John.

"Obviously, I wouldn't expect anything else."

Jodie said, "Louise told me she wouldn't be surprised if the directors call in the next couple of days to discuss some more projects."

"No way! That's awesome." Sophie leant over to hug Jodie again. He loved that the two of them got on so well.

"Yeah, but we will see what happens." Jodie shrugged it off as she always did. One day she would believe in herself and her abilities, but until then Tony would make sure that he always told her how amazing she was. "What's new with you?"

Sophie shrugged, but John cut in on her behalf. "Sophie was just telling me about a competition or something, weren't you, Soph?"

"Oh, it's nothing." Sophie batted them away.

"No, go on. Spill it." Jodie nudged her.

"Well, I saw a competition in a magazine, and I don't know what came over me, but I thought what the hell? Just enter it. You don't have anything to lose. I mean, I never win at these things, and at some point in my life I have to get lucky, don't I?"

"What was the competition for?" Tony asked.

"To go to the Best of British Talent Awards night. Anyway, I got a phone call and I won."

"You didn't." John looked gobsmacked. "You don't even win at the school raffle!"

"I know! But that's not even the best bit. I'll be having a makeover done by the magazine—make-up, outfit, hair, the works. Then a photo shoot and a twenty-minute meet and greet with Josh Heart."

Jodie gasped. "No way, that's incredible." Tony and John looked at her blankly. "Oh come on, you two know every bit of gossip in this village but you don't know who Josh Heart is?"

"Do you get a plus one?" John asked, his eyes on another glass.

"Yes," she replied timidly.

Tony opened his mouth to speak, and then he remembered what Jodie had said before. He wanted to tell Sophie yet again that Scott didn't deserve her, and that she would be so much happier if she found someone else. But instead he said, "We're happy for you, Soph. Aren't we John?" He widened his eyes at John trying to communicate their new plan without saying anything.

John narrowed his eyes at him, his face screwed up, completely perplexed. Tony nodded at him silently and John seemed to cotton on. "Course we are. When you're happy, we're happy."

Tony smiled at him, and then turned to Sophie who was looking between them both, equally as confused as John was. He had no doubt that Sophie would come to the decision on her own, but he bloody well hoped it was sooner rather than later.

He turned to Jodie who had a big smile on her face. She squeezed his hand, obviously proud of him. They sat for a while, talking to his best friends and laughing. Life was turning out pretty great.

Jodie got undressed in Tony's bedroom—no, *their* bedroom—and put on her leggings and a baggy top. She was exhausted, not just from today and the opening of the show homes, but the months of hard work, running around and sleepless nights that had led up to it. But it couldn't have gone better, and it was all worth it. Sure, it wasn't perfect and she could see the small errors she had made along the way, but no one else saw them, and everyone had been so complimentary.

It was all finally coming together. She hadn't worked a shift at The Dog for a couple of months now as she'd needed to concentrate on the show homes and a few retail clients had started to trickle through. Tony and Micha knew she was around if they really needed her last minute to cover for anyone, but they seemed to have got in a permanent replacement, so she no longer felt guilty about leaving them in the lurch.

She opened one of the bedroom windows, letting the evening summer breeze through the bedroom. As it always did, her little cottage caught her eye, the house empty and closed up. A few weeks back, they had finally agreed that she would move into Tony's house. It made sense, what with him being that bit closer to the pub, and him living in Winton Green for longer. But the biggest reason was that she still couldn't shake the fact that being here altogether just felt like home. Even when all three of them had gone and stayed in her cottage, it didn't feel right, more like a holiday home. So now this was *their* place.

Although she wasn't living there anymore, she was still using her house as her office space. After all, Tony's back bedroom that he used as an office was overrun and there was no way they were both fitting in there without a good clear out. And she had taken the opportunity to show a few potential clients around now that it was fully decorated. Everyone she had done that with so far had loved that and she had won all of their contracts. So for now, it was staying as her office-come-show-home. Very over the top, but it seemed to be working. And then in the near future, maybe it would turn out to be a holiday let, but right now it was staying as it was.

Finally ready, she headed downstairs, ready to snuggle on the sofa with her feet up and watch whatever junk happened to be on TV that night. Maybe it wasn't the most exciting evening plan, but as long as she had Tony and Max with her, she couldn't have asked for anything better.

When she reached the bottom of the stairs, she was met by

a wall of hot air. Looking around the room, she spotted the crackling fire in the fireplace and then Tony, laid out before it on the rug in his smart jeans and shirt.

"Tony!" she cried. "It's boiling in here." She shook her head laughing at his audacity. They had only just managed to get a chimney sweep to come yesterday, just before autumn arrived and they would want to start using the fireplace.

"I couldn't resist," he told her. "I've been wanting to use it for ages—ever since you said about it, and I could see the dirty little thoughts flying through your mind. I've been counting down the days to try it out."

She joined him on the rug amongst the cushions he had piled up to lie on. The heat was sweltering this close to the fire. Pulling off her shirt so she was just in her bra, she lay on him, kissing him passionately.

Groaning into her mouth, he stroked her bare back, pulling at the clasp on her bra to undo it. "It's too hot in here," he said, bringing her straps down and releasing her breasts.

"You should put the fire out then," she moaned as he cupped and sucked her nipple.

"Never," he breathed.

The End

Want to hear more from Tony and Jodie?
Sign up for Marie Harper Wright's Exclusive Reader List for a Bonus Epilogue.

https://www.marieharperwright.com/exclusive-reader-list

Next in the series…

The worst thing that could happen after a one night stand would be for the whole world to find out about it.

Josh Heart is an icon. Known worldwide for his music, songwriting and being the most eligible bachelor in Britain. Somehow he'd managed to hide the biggest mistake of his life. A mistake that risked not only his heart, but also someone's life. So now he lived by one rule. He didn't date fans. And he would never break it, not even for Sophie Ward who stole his breath away the moment he saw her. No, he had rules…and they were there to save her life.

Primary school teacher Sophie Ward couldn't believe her luck. She was finally within reaching distance of her long awaited promotion. And to top it all off she was attending the hottest award ceremony with a meet and greet with the Josh Heart. But her future career depended on her having boundaries… and keeping them. There was no way she would jeopardise her promotion for a man. Even if that man was Josh Heart.

Twenty minutes is all they were meant to have with each other. But can they deny their desire to spend one more second together? Or will fear destroy their future?

Found out in book 2 of this steamy romance series set in the quaint village of Winton Green.

Sign up to Marie Harper Wright's Exclusive Reader List to be the first to receive update's on upcoming releases and bonus content
https://www.marieharperwright.com/exclusive-reader-list

ABOUT THE AUTHOR

Marie Harper Wright lives and writes in Kent, UK with her husband and two boys. She wants to transport you to English countryside where you can forget all your troubles and lose yourself in picturesque villages with sassy heroines and loving heroes.

Find out more about Marie Harper Wright by signing up to her newsletter or by following her on social media.

www.marieharperwright.com

Printed in Great Britain
by Amazon

14078400R00144